D1650206

A Dyeing Shame

A Myrtle Clover Cozy Mystery, Volume 3

Elizabeth Spann Craig

Published by Elizabeth Craig, 2019.

A DYEING SHAME

First edition. March 4, 2019.

Written by Elizabeth Spann Craig.

For my family and in memory of my grandmothers.

Chapter One

"**C**ongratulate me, Red! And join me in a toast. To driving!" Myrtle took a swig from her wine glass.

Her son, Red, rolled his eyes at his wife as she kicked open the back door with their toddler on one hip and a bag of groceries on the other. He resisted the urge to hang up the phone on his mother. "What for, Mama? Finally beat Mrs. Meyers playing Scrabble?"

"You know I always let that poor woman win. No, I just came back from the Department of Motor Vehicles. They renewed my driver's license for ten more years!"

Red, taking the grocery bag from Elaine, dropped the phone. Picking it up, he said, "But Mama, you haven't even regularly driven a car for at least five years!"

"That didn't seem to bother the DMV one bit. Besides, I do get some driving practice in from time to time. Miles drove me there this morning. I had a fantastic picture taken."

"Why on earth do you even *need* to drive? I'm happy to drive you anywhere you need to go. You don't even *own* a car. Shoot, Mama, downtown is only a few blocks away anyhow."

"I'll drive Caroline Wilson's car. She told me just the other day that she wants it warmed up from time to time."

Red battled a rising tide of panic. As Bradley, North Carolina Chief of Police, he took his duty ensuring public safety very seriously.

Having his octogenarian mother terrorizing the citizenry in a borrowed 1978 Cadillac Fleetwood didn't fit his vision.

Elaine watched as her husband's face grew redder with his rising blood pressure. Elaine, ten years younger than forty-five year old Red, thought of his mom as more of a surrogate grandmother than a mother-in-law. This kept Myrtle from really getting on Elaine's nerves. Out of concern for his mother's safety (so he said), Red had made another ill-advised attempt to orchestrate his mother to the Greener Pastures Retirement Home last year. After a Clash-of-the-Titans-style fight, Myrtle won. Naturally.

"Tell you what, Mama. How about I bring you lunch? To, uh, celebrate. Elaine just came back from the store and she's got some..." He looked at Elaine urgently as she pulled up various foodstuffs from the depths of the grocery bags. "...fresh-baked rye bread and Cajun roast beef. Mmm...and a melon bowl, too. If you've got some barbeque chips, and I bet you do, then we've got lunch." Cementing the deal, Red hung up and scowled at the phone.

"Got to figure out what's going on with Mama. Today it's cars. What's next? Motorcycles? You know how she gets these fixations." Red checked the wall clock. "Mama must've been at the DMV when it opened because it's hardly even lunchtime now. She's even opened up a bottle of wine."

Elaine's frown wrinkled her forehead. "She must really have been bored to hang out at the DMV all morning."

Red pictured his mother in a jaunty riding hat, tooting her horn and yoo-hooing to any pedestrians she knew. He groaned and grabbed a few of the groceries. Giving Elaine a quick kiss, he hurried out the door, straightening his uniform as he stomped out toward a small house directly across the road.

Myrtle peered through her window as Red, clutching a grocery bag, walked briskly out of his house. She smiled. This was a record for her—a two-minute phone conversation netted her both a free lunch *and* a visit with her son.

She watched his progress with a critical eye. He was a nice-looking boy, even if that scowl messed up his features. He was still a boy to her, even though the red hair that spawned his nickname was now liberally sprinkled with gray.

Red entered without knocking, headed into the kitchen, and unloaded the grocery bag. Myrtle's growling stomach reproachfully reminded her that she hadn't eaten all day.

"What've you got lined up at work today?" asked Myrtle, reaching for the bread.

Red rolled his eyes. "Mrs. Peterson wants me to drop by again after lunch."

"More neighborhood kids cutting across her lawn?"

"Either that or the suspicious prowler lurking behind her hydrangeas again. Or she might be complaining that deaf, old Mr. Smith has his TV turned up too loud again next door. Could be anything. She just likes checking in with me every day."

Myrtle sniffed. "She's probably bored and wants company."

"Don't be smug, Mama. You're sounding pretty bored yourself. But why, I don't know. I thought you were still busy beating everyone in town at bridge."

Myrtle shook her head. "The thrill has gone, Red. No one will play against me. They think I'm a card shark. It's the unfortunate downside of tremendous success."

"You could try another card game," said Red. At her questioning look, he innocently asked, "Poker?"

Myrtle drew up and peered down her nose at Red. Her affected patrician Southern lady look clashed with her big boned, solid frame. "I'll pretend you didn't go there," she said regally.

"Or bunko or Crazy 8s or Old Maid. Just stay out of trouble, please. Don't get bored. Remember the last time you got bored? You got all tangled up in local politics...and you remember how well *that* turned out."

"For your information, Red, sit-ins are an excellent way to draw attention to a cause. Civil disobedience and all that."

"Sit-ins are not ideal for arthritic elderly ladies, Mama. Miss Hanover is still molded in prime sit-in position this very day."

"Next time we'll bring chairs." Myrtle frowned. "Old age is a terrible thing."

"It beats the alternative," said Red.

"I'm not so sure."

"What about 'Grow old along with me, the best is yet to be'?" Red looked pleased with himself with summoning up the line. Growing up with an English teacher for a mom, he'd certainly heard plenty of quotations. She sure hoped some of it had stuck.

"Robert Browning was a mere child," said Myrtle with a sniff. "What did he know? Anne Bradstreet had it right:

My memory is short, and braine is dry.

My gray haires doth flourish now.
And back, once straight, begins apace to bow.

Red studied her. "Your back looks plenty straight to me. The brain and gray hair are a different story, though. What's with the quotes? Seems like you've been doing them a lot lately."

"*Quotations.* I'm just trying to keep my brain from going to mush. Which is hard, considering there's a tremendous lack of intellectual stimulation here in Bradley."

"What about your book club?" Red seemed to be trying to hide a smile.

"Please! No mention of that horrific book club."

"Did it ever switch back from being a supper club to being a book club again? I've lost track of its different incarnations," said Red.

"Yes, it has. And I think we're supposed to be reading some dreadful novel this month. I've about given up on it. The books are all *Heather's Lost Love* or that sort of thing." Myrtle gave an exasperated sigh.

"Maybe you should take up art."

"Is art something you just *take up*? Isn't it more like a calling?" asked Myrtle.

"I've no idea. Either way, Elaine just got called. She's been busily painting for the last few days now."

Myrtle frowned. "She's painting *canvasses*? Not rooms? I didn't realize she could paint."

Red said delicately, "Well, that remains to be seen. All I'm saying is that she's painting. And from what I could see of the canvas, I think you might be the subject of one of her masterpieces."

He checked his watch. "Sorry to end our fascinating lunch discussion, but I've got to run check on Mrs. Peterson now. Enjoy your afternoon." He gave his mother a peck on the cheek. "Why don't you visit Elaine? You could play with Jack for a while. Or take a look at Elaine's painting."

"Maybe after *Tomorrow's Promise*. I missed it yesterday and haven't watched my recording yet. And I should probably pick up some veggies at the farmer's market, too. Is Elaine doing anything a little later?"

"I don't think so. Later probably works better anyway, since it's almost Jack's naptime now." He opened her pantry and grabbed a couple of chocolate chip cookies. "Glad you still keep the pantry stocked for me," he said with a wink and left.

Myrtle smiled and pulled out a cookie for herself. Picking up the remote, she plopped down on the sofa and clicked on the television. Life, relationships, and routines might change, but her soap opera was forever.

After an hour of following most of the convoluted subplots on *Tomorrow's Promise*, she turned off the TV, grabbed her cane, and made the short walk on tree-lined streets to the farmer's market. She sighed. Same old brick stores. Same old people. Some things never changed. And sometimes she wished they would.

She walked up to the small commons area near City Hall, where farmers sold produce on summertime Saturdays. Shoot. She'd forgotten her bag. And the corn was looking awfully good. There were *peaches* here, too! Where had those come from? Surely there shouldn't be any peaches anymore.

Agnes Walker, wearing a large hat to protect her genteel features, held a wicker basket of vegetables as she peered at some beans. She studied those snap beans with the same careful consideration she applied to everything in life.

"You're looking rather sour this morning," observed Agnes, catching sight of her friend.

Myrtle frowned. "I forgot my produce bag."

"That's it?" Agnes raised her eyebrows. "That's your only complaint?"

"And I'm...a little bored."

Agnes dropped the snap beans into a paper bag. "Surely that's not allowed. I thought only children were permitted boredom." She pointedly looked Myrtle up and down from her carefully arranged thinning hair to her sensible SAS shoes. Myrtle certainly didn't qualify as a child.

"I've earned the right to boredom," said Myrtle. "I've sampled all the entertainment for the elderly in this town. Bingo and bridge. Mad Hatter teas and early bird supper deals. Book clubs and the historical society. I've been around a long, long time. I've done it all, seen it all, and now I'm bored with it all. Welcome to Bradley," she said grouchily. "Maybe I'll work for the tourism board."

Agnes considered the problem while the farmer weighed her beans. "There's always travel," she offered.

"Who would go with me? Red and Elaine are busy with Jack. And all my ancient friends are dropping like flies." She brightened. "Say Agnes, what if you and I—"

"Allow me to stop you right there. My traveling days are over. Been there, done that. Sitting still for long distances in a car makes me stiff."

"There are airplanes," explained Myrtle, in case Agnes hadn't heard the news.

"I'm aware of that," said Agnes with dignity. "I don't care for the cramped powder rooms. No, Myrtle, I'm finished traveling. There's nothing much I care to see. Any family who wants a visit can come to me."

Myrtle sighed. "Fine. Well, if you won't travel, then maybe you and I can at least go over to Greener Pastures tomorrow and visit. The Sunday dinner there is decent."

"That's awfully altruistic of you." There was a suspicious gleam in Agnes' eyes. "Are you sure you're not just wanting to prance into Greener Pastures to show off your vim and vigor?"

"It's definitely the *food* that's the draw." Myrtle set her chin.

"I heard you complaining about the food there only last week! I simply can't figure you out, Myrtle. It's actually quite lovely that Bradley is as quiet and serene as it is. And you're doing things like tapping your foot at the curb while waiting for the mailman."

Myrtle flushed.

"Then last week you called me to ponder the inconsistencies of the garbage collection service. You've got too much time on your hands," said Agnes.

"Have you been hanging out with Red? There's no reason a citizen shouldn't reasonably expect her mail delivered or garbage picked up at the same time each day or week," said Myrtle.

Agnes smiled. "Still rating the weather forecasters' predictions and emailing them reports of their mistakes?"

"And miserably error-prone crackpots they are, too!"

"There's no reason for you to be bored, anyway," said Agnes. "There's plenty of local intrigue."

Myrtle's ears pricked up. "Go on," she urged.

Agnes' natural discretion seemed to be warring with her urge to gossip. Then discretion won out. Rats. Agnes clamped her lips in a tight line to keep the gossip from bursting out. She said mysteriously, "You'll find out tomorrow morning at the Beauty Box."

"Has Tammy lost her mind again?" Tammy was the hairdresser and former confidante of the ladies who saw her. But drinking made Tammy loose-lipped, and cats were flying out of bags with amazing regularity in recent weeks.

"You'll see."

"Too bad Tammy's going downhill like this. Are...she and Connor still going out?" She tried to make sure that only friendly concern showed in her expression. Connor, as Agnes' only child and her pride and joy, had been having an on-again off-again relationship with Tammy. Agnes either didn't hear her or didn't choose to hear her. "See you tomorrow," she called as she walked away.

Both Elaine and toddler Jack beamed at Myrtle when they opened the door. Jack raced to grab a toy dump truck to show his grandmother. Myrtle settled on the lofty perch of the sofa; she'd learned her lesson a week ago when she got stuck on the floor playing with Jack. Getting down there wasn't bad, but getting back up again thirty minutes later was a different story.

Elaine joined them in the living room, regarding Myrtle with all the eagerness of a stranded stay-at-home mom. "So! Any excitement?"

"You and I are in the same boat, aren't we? I may have some gossip soon, though, courtesy of the Beauty Box. Apparently that's where all the action is."

Elaine put a protective hand to her hair. "I'll let you get the low-down, then. Tammy butchered my hair last time and I haven't been back since. Jack could have done a better job with it. Remember? That's how I ended up getting this bob. Red liked me with long hair better, and he's still steamed with Tammy."

Maybe so. But the bob suited Elaine's heart-shaped face and high-lighted her high cheekbones. Red was a lucky man.

"I love your hair," said Myrtle. "But you're right to steer clear of the Beauty Box. Tammy's completely unreliable right now."

"It's too bad. Tammy gave the best scalp massages. I felt so relaxed when I left there." Elaine gave a wistful sigh. "What kind of trouble is happening at the Beauty Box?"

"Agnes wasn't too forthcoming, unfortunately. But from what I've seen, Tammy is hitting the sauce with a vengeance now."

Elaine watched Jack ram the dump truck into a toy ambulance. "Hmm. Tammy drinking? That could have dangerous consequences. She knows all the secrets of every woman in town. It'd be like a bartender spilling secrets."

Myrtle nodded. "Or a priest. Tammy knows all the dirt on everyone. Even if they don't tell her their secrets, she's got some kind of instinct for them. That was fine when she was professional enough to keep secrets. But once she threw alcohol in the mix?" Myrtle shrugged. "Anyway, that's the news. I'll give you the scoop tomorrow."

"Aren't you worried that Tammy will make you look like Bride of Frankenstein?"

Myrtle thoughtfully fingered her hair. As usual, it stood up on end like Einstein's. "Not really. My hair has a mind of its own."

"Tammy has a new girl at the shop, doesn't she? Kat—she's her niece, right? I wonder if she does a better job with hair."

Kat's hair was dyed fuchsia and she sported rings through her nose, bellybutton, and probably other places Myrtle didn't want to know about. So far the ladies of Bradley appeared reticent to entrust their precious locks to Kat's care. But with Tammy incapacitated, Kat's clientele might be on the rise.

"She probably knows what's trendy. You could always try her, I guess." Myrtle stood up. "I'm going home to put my feet up for a while. The DMV will sure take it out of you."

Elaine snapped her fingers. "Before you go, I wanted to give you something." She pushed open the kitchen door, and Myrtle saw that it had been transformed into a sort of transient art studio. Not a very organized one, either. Elaine leafed through a short stack of canvasses on the table. "Let's see. Here it is!"

Elaine held up a painting that made Myrtle immediately want to cover her eyes. "This is for you, Myrtle! What do you think?"

She was having a visceral reaction to the painting. A small, pained cry escaped from her, which Elaine fortunately attributed to delight. "See? This is you. And this is Miles. And you're both surrounded with books!" Elaine smiled at her.

Myrtle, summoning incredible willpower, beamed right back at her. "I'm speechless. I'm...wow." She nodded wordlessly at the painting. So, that blobby thing was her? And the other thing was Miles? But Miles looked more like a woman than she did! And the books seemed to meld into each other with more muddy blobbing.

"I thought you might need something for your mantel that represented your life with books and maybe also the friendship you found in books. And Miles is a literary friend!" said Elaine.

It all made wonderful sense. Except for the fact that what was being proposed to decorate the mantel was a complete abomination.

She hugged Elaine tightly. "Yes! It's an amazing painting, Elaine. But I think it might be selfish of me to hog it. Miles and I could *share* the painting. Maybe a week at my house and a week at his."

Elaine said in an excited voice, "What a nice idea! Because, really, it's a painting about friendship. The friendship between the two of you and your friendship with books."

"Exactly." Miles wore glasses, after all. He could simply take them off when it was his turn with the painting. Without his glasses, it would probably seem like a lovely, vague Monet.

Jack came over to hug her bye before resuming wrecking his trucks into each other. Myrtle smiled bravely as she gingerly took the painting in one hand, grabbed her cane with the other, and gratefully took her leave.

Chapter Two

Myrtle was ready especially early for her hair appointment the next morning. Lured by the prospect of juicy gossip or, God-willing, a scene, Myrtle set aside her bowl of Grape Nuts, haphazardly applied lipstick while pulling on a pastel pantsuit, and grabbed her cane.

Before heading in the direction of the Beauty Box, she walked a couple of doors down to Miles' house. She placed Elaine's painting in a bag on Miles' porch with a sticky note that said *Thinking of You.* Myrtle hurried off without knocking on his door.

She smiled with satisfaction as she approached the salon, always relieved that Tammy hadn't yielded to hyperactive punning when naming the shop. The town already had a barber shop called Hair Today, Gone Tomorrow and a beauty parlor called Hair-raisers. Puns made Myrtle queasy.

The inside of the shop was just as satisfactory as the outside. The ancient window unit spat out ice-cold air with a determined drone, and the domed hairdryers noisily competed with it. Ladies hollered over the ruckus, and it required skill and concentration to selectively eavesdrop.

The salon's décor was eclectic and, although Tammy had decorated it in her pre-drinking days, that fact wasn't evident. Bulbous, multi-colored Christmas lights covered the walls year-round, and large posters prominently displayed unlikely-looking hair models. Red and yellow curtains clashed with avocado-colored vinyl drying chairs. Faux terra cotta walls completed the Spanish bordello look. The salon was designed as a duplex with the beauty parlor in one section and Tammy's living quarters in the other. The manicurist also lived in one of the bedrooms in the other side of the duplex.

Myrtle immediately saw that Tammy was in rare form. She was gesticulating wildly with a liquor bottle and laughing hoarsely at a joke no one else apparently found funny. Instead of tranquil ladies settled in for their weekly soul baring and beautification, the shop was full of pinched faces. Agnes Walker looked grim as she got a manicure. The most anxious of the faces belonged to the victim of the moment, Bootsie Davenport. She sat stiffly in the chair with a martyred expression on her face. Judge Beauregard Davenport's wife and local socialite, Bootsie had no desire to sacrifice her coif to Tammy's binge-drinking.

"If y'all would loosen up and have a little cocktail, we'd all have a lot more fun." Tammy knocked over a few bottles of hair product in accidental emphasis.

Making her grand entrance, Myrtle quoted dramatically, "*I lived on rum, I tell you. It's been meat and drink, and man and wife, to me.*" Resurrecting these quotations from the depths of her memory was actually very validating. Red thought she needed to be shipped to a retirement home. Pooh!

Her arrival was greeted by an unusual sigh of relief at the distraction. "Myrtle!" said Agnes in a fond voice before guessing, "Kipling?"

"Stevenson," said Myrtle. "*Treasure Island.*"

Agnes smiled. "I'm so glad you escaped being locked away at Greener Pastures Retirement Home, Myrtle. Whatever would we have done without you?"

"I won't be an inmate at their asylum," answered Myrtle dryly.

Bootsie said, "Asylum? Greener Pastures is a wonderful Home, Miss Myrtle. My own dear Mama is out there and is happy as a clam."

"I stand corrected." As soon as Bootsie was distracted by her ringing cell phone, Myrtle muttered to Agnes, "She's happy as a clam because she's half-baked. She entered the dining hall in nightie and robe and commenced a vigorous tooth-brushing when I visited Mirabelle the other night."

Prissy Daniels peered myopically into her tatty, cavernous handbag for her checkbook. Her just-styled hair looked pretty good, considering Tammy's present state. Pretty good for Prissy, anyway. Myrtle suspected that Prissy was the prototype for Old-Maid cards. She fit the part, right down to her knobby knees. Prissy patted her just-permed hair gingerly, made a vague goodbye and left the shop.

"Bye, Pris!" Tammy hollered as the door closed. She gave a derisive snort. "That Prissy. *Bless* her heart. She sure isn't what she seems." She winked at a frowning Agnes and said, "Prissy looks all prim and proper with her pearls and twin-sets. But you wouldn't believe the real Prissy if I told you."

"Then don't," suggested Agnes in a frosty voice.

Myrtle glowered. She'd have to have a talk with Agnes about stifling Tammy. The whole point of going to the beauty parlor was to learn gossip. What could she be thinking?

"I won't. I'm no blabbermouth. Never have been! Although I could tell some real tales on Miss Priss—"

Bootsie's loud cough interrupted Tammy. Prissy stood in the doorway, gaping at Tammy.

"Forget your specs again, Prissy?" asked Tammy. "I was just explaining to Bootsie here that you're not as demure as you make out. Isn't that right?" She gave a raucous bellow of laughter.

Prissy bleated something unintelligible, her long face turning blotchy red as she snatched up her glasses and fumbled her way out the door.

"Tammy," said Agnes in a stern voice, "I know you've been struggling with alcohol again—"

"Sure have!" interrupted Tammy cheerfully as she waved a comb in the direction of the bottle, standing in the midst of a colorful array of mousses, shampoos and hair sprays. "Want some? Never mind, I'm not sharing, anyway."

Agnes glared at Tammy disapprovingly. "Why are you drinking like this when you and Connor seem so happy together? I just don't understand what precipitated this."

"Ah, Connor. Mama's pride and joy, isn't he?"

Agnes ignored the jab. "You should consider getting some help."

"No thanks, Mrs. Walker. I'm getting plenty of help from the bottle."

It did seem like a strange time for Tammy to fall off the wagon. She'd had an amicable divorce from former husband Bo. Her shop was doing well, her niece lived nearby, and she was dating a good guy. Did she weather the hard times easier than the good ones?

Myrtle turned a critical eye on Tammy. She'd been pretty, although lately she'd let herself go. Dark roots and straggling gray hairs replaced the blond highlights she usually sported. The neat smock she'd worn over her clothes was nowhere in evidence, probably because the ratty sweat suit she wore didn't need protecting. A cigarette dangled out the corner of Tammy's mouth. From time to time, a column of ash fell into Bootsie's curls before disappearing.

The waiting area was full of old magazines that hadn't been replaced by new ones in months. Tammy was really letting the place slide. Myrtle leafed through one magazine that she'd already read several times before tossing it back down. "Any excitement?" she asked the other women.

Tammy snickered. "There's always something going on in Bradley. Isn't that right, Bootsie?"

Bootsie gave Tammy a hard look through squinty eyes in the mirror before she answered brightly, "Absolutely! I'm on a committee to plan the next church fundraiser. It's going to be a festival. It'll be the third week in October, so mark your calendars now."

Dina, the anxious-faced manicurist, nervously dabbed polish on Agnes' nails. She said in her squeaky voice, "A festival. That sounds very nice."

A church festival wasn't the kind of excitement that Tammy was likely referring to.

Tammy's assistant beautician and niece, Kat Roberts, walked in while everyone stared. Kat was a tattoo-sporting, pierced, pink-haired anomaly in the town. "We were just talking about Bradley," said Bootsie to Kat. "Not quite as exciting here as it was in New York, is it?"

Kat shrugged. "No, but it doesn't matter to me. I've had enough excitement."

Myrtle remembered hearing that Kat's move was precipitated by her mother's arrest for dealing drugs. Her father ran off long ago, and Aunt Tammy was the only family Kat had left. Tammy had driven her to North Carolina and promptly enrolled her in beauty school.

But Bradley, North Carolina, might not be quite ready for Kat. Her style sense turned heads, but it hadn't inspired confidence in the Beauty Box crowd. Kat didn't seem to have any regulars yet.

Myrtle patted her hair. As usual, it was standing on end. Surely Kat couldn't make it any worse than it already was. Or as bad as a drunken Tammy might make it. "Since Tammy is tied up with Bootsie, could you do a wash and set for me, Kat?"

Kat's tough features brightened and she spun a chair around. "Have a seat!" Kat was actually pretty when she smiled. Was that a shiny pimple on her nose, though? Oh. A nose stud. Myrtle sighed.

Tammy stubbed out her cigarette, then stumbled and nearly stabbed the shrieking Bootsie with her clippers. "You're fine, you're fine," she muttered to Bootsie. Kat shot her aunt a disapproving look, and Tammy put her hands on her hips. "What is this, the Ladies' Temperance Society? You're not some goody-two-shoes are you, Kat?"

Kat stayed stoically silent as she competently scrubbed Myrtle's hair, but her hands shook with the effort of holding back.

The air in the room was heavy with disapproval. Tammy shrugged. "Shouldn't matter what I do as long as I cut hair okay. I'm not breaking any laws." She blanketed Bootsie's hair with enough Aqua Net to annihilate the remainder of the ozone layer. "I'm a decent, good-hearted—would somebody *get* that phone?" She roared as the devil-possessed instrument rang and rang. Probably women canceling their appointments in droves. Dina, the mousy manicurist, obediently snatched up the receiver.

Tammy pieced together her scattered thoughts. "I'm a good Christian woman." She whipped her head around in an unsuccessful attempt to pin down the source of the derisive snort behind her. "I'm giving Kat a fresh start." Kat shot her a look that said where she could put the fresh start. "And I even put her up here with me until Kat got her own place."

"And remember little Dina, too," Tammy ordered, gesturing to the timid manicurist who had put down the phone and was again nervously filing Agnes' nails. "She had to run away from that no-good cretin of a husband. When she needed a place to go, who took her in? Did *y'all* take her in? Give her a place to stay? Food to eat? Nope. It was me!"

Agnes gave a delicate cough. "Dina does have feelings, you know, Tammy. Don't talk about her like she's not in the room. She's not some stray kitten."

Dina pushed her glasses up her nose and shook her head, frizzy curls bobbing emphatically. "Oh, I don't mind, Miss Agnes. Tammy's been a lifesaver and I'm just so very grateful."

"I'm sure you are, dear..."

"The point is," interrupted Tammy loudly, "that Dina knows I'm a good person. Doing nails and being my roommate are much better than being bullied by your husband. I should know—I put up with Bo for so long. Dina, grab that hairspray for me." Bootsie looked pained at the suggestion of more hairspray. Her hair might never move again.

Dina gave the bottle to Tammy, who glanced over at the manicure Dina was giving Agnes. Dina's brow furrowed anxiously as she waited for Tammy's approval. Tammy shrugged and started spraying another half bottle of hairspray on Bootsie's head. Dina's face fell. The poor thing had gone from one bully to another.

"Never mind," said Tammy, slurring a little. "I don't care who knows I'm a good person or not. I don't care about any of you. I'm writing you out of my will."

Agnes looked over at Myrtle and rolled her eyes. "Tammy, none of us are probably even in your will. We're not worried."

"Well, you sure aren't. But Kat and Dina are...or were." Tammy had that sly, trouble-making expression on her face again.

"Go ahead, Tammy. I've never asked for anything from you. Whatever you've done for me has been your idea," said Kat in a grim voice.

Kat's cheeks were flushed with anger. Myrtle cleared her throat, the smell of Aqua Net making her woozy. "Kat, how do you like Bradley so far?"

Kat relaxed a little and flashed the surprisingly pretty smile again. "So far, so good. It's cool to have my own place. I'm renting a house and have a yard for the first time. Yards were tough to come by in the city."

"You probably used public transportation in New York. Did you have to take Driver's Ed. when you moved here?"

Kat said briskly, "Sure did. But I had to learn so I could drive over to the beauty school. The closest one was twenty miles away. Once I passed the driver's test, I got my bike."

Myrtle puzzled over this for a minute. "Why'd you get a license if you were biking everywhere?"

Kat frowned, then laughed. "It's not a bicycle: it's a motorcycle. A Harley. I've always wanted one, so I got a used one. Runs like a dream."

A pink-haired Harley driver with a nose stud. Myrtle offered a belated supplication to the hair gods. But soon she noticed that her hair looked better than it had in years. Kat appraised her work with a critical eye and gently combed Myrtle's hair for the finishing touch. "Okay?" asked Kat.

"Much better than okay," said Myrtle. "I do believe you've won my business, Kat. Put me down on your calendar for next week." Satisfaction gleamed in Kat's eyes. Myrtle saw something else there, too: a little raw ambition. Tammy shot her niece a cold look. It sure didn't look like Tammy was rooting for Kat to succeed.

Tammy dropped a mirror in Bootsie's lap so she could look at the back of her head. "Here you go, sweetheart. Another Tammy masterpiece, just for you."

Bootsie patted her hair gingerly. "Isn't it poofier than it usually is?"

Tammy flushed blotchy red. "It's the same way you always want it, Bootsie. What's the problem?'

"I don't know. It's like an old-lady do today."

Tammy hissed viciously. "Is it? Well, you've always been happy to look like an old lady before. Why is today any different? Let me guess. You're wanting to impress your young man."

Bootsie choked out a strangled laugh. "I don't care at all about impressing Justin. He's away at college and doesn't care what his old Mama looks like."

"I don't *mean* Justin," Tammy sneered.

Every ear in the Beauty Box strained to hear over the wall unit as Bootsie gritted through clenched teeth, "You'd better watch yourself, or I'll prosecute you for libel."

Tammy drawled, "Can't be libel when it's true."

Whatever Bootsie planned to say was cut off as her cell phone, with a rapping ringtone that made Myrtle's eyebrows rise, started ringing again. Bootsie dug a couple of bills out of her wallet and slammed them on the counter, answering her phone with a barking, "Hel-*lo*!" as she left.

"And y'all think *I* have a temper," muttered Tammy, shaking her head. "Gotta get some air. Kat, you'll manage things, right?"

"Better than you can, Tammy."

Maybe it was the truth in that statement that so infuriated Tammy. Tammy picked up the mirror and hurled it down. The Beauty Box became silent as glass splintered across the floor. Tammy froze, superstitious fear giving her a sober moment. "Seven years of bad luck," she grated. Shaking it off, she slouched unsteadily out the door. A collective sigh of relief wafted through the beauty parlor. Myrtle peered through the window to ensure that Tammy was walking and not driving. She asked, "When did Tammy turn into the Wicked Witch of the South?"

Agnes said, "Well, Connor says alcohol is something she's always struggled with. Both her parents were hard drinkers."

"In less than an hour, she managed to offend just about everyone here."

Kat's voice was studiously casual. "Sorry about the way she was acting today. I guess you know that Tammy isn't usually this bad."

"Of course she's not! She wouldn't have a customer left, if she were."

Agnes checked her nails to see if they were dry. "She took some stabs at me too today. You're the only one who escaped unscathed, Myrtle."

"I'm too dull to give her any ammo," said Myrtle. "We all used to treat her like our personal shrink. Tammy heard all the secrets."

Agnes said morosely, "And now she's a loose cannon. We'll have to find our confidantes elsewhere."

Dina spilled some nail polish on the table and started dabbing it up with a paper towel. She said unhappily, "Tammy will be okay soon. She's just working through her problems."

Kat snorted. "I know you're trying to be a good friend, but we can't excuse Tammy from acting out. Tammy doesn't have *real* problems. Tammy is Tammy's problem. The drinking will kill her, though. One way or another."

Chapter Three

Prissy Daniels pulled out her Wedgwood teacup from her china cabinet—what was the use of having good china if you didn't use it every day? —and carefully measured cream and sugar into her tea. Something a little stronger would have better steadied her nerves, but tea was the strongest beverage to ever pass through her thin lips.

The delicate cup rattled against its saucer in her shaking hands. What a shock! Tammy had styled Prissy's fluffy hairdo for ten years. Never had Tammy been so indiscreet.

Teaching Sunday school each week and presiding as preschool director at the church gave Prissy real prestige in Bradley, North Carolina. She was a moral compass for the town's children. It was upsetting to realize that Tammy had the capacity to destroy Prissy's image as the sweet, innocuous local spinster.

Bootsie Davenport, feeling like the Peach Festival Queen again, smiled contentedly at her "young man." When she was with her husband, Beauregard Davenport, she just felt old. In Beauregard's face she saw her own wrinkles reflected back at her. He was an old man, but he was intent on living a lot longer than she'd reckoned on.

Bootsie's companion trailed his hand on her shoulder and brought her back to the present. Trying to focus, she pulled away from him. He raised his eyebrows at her. "I wanted to tell you," she said uncertainly, "that there may be some gossip going around about us."

"What?" He sat up a little.

"My hairdresser is dishing dirt on everybody. But nobody pays any attention; Tammy's got a drinking problem."

"I thought you understood not to tell anyone about us." There was a hard note in his voice.

Bootsie sighed. "I know, sweetheart. But it's hard...so hard not to share this with anybody."

His attractive features softened a bit. "You know how much I care about you. But if Beauregard finds out about us, our love nest is finished. He'll make sure you don't have a penny."

"But we'd still have each other. We'd make it turn out all right." The young man shook his head slowly, and Bootsie flinched as the hard reality of his motives sank in.

She wouldn't give this up. Bootsie tried everything in her pursuit of youth: surgery, expensive moisturizers, and *trompe d'oeil* makeup. Her hair and clothes remained conservative, as a sop to her husband's sensibilities. This relationship made her feel younger than anything else she'd tried.

She still had to be careful. Judging was exactly what Beauregard would do if he realized she was cheating. She knew the sentence, too—divorce from Judge Davenport and all of his many worldly possessions. She had too many years invested to suffer that fate.

Bootsie said, "I'll make sure Tammy shuts up, then. She'll have to."

"That's my girl," he said and pulled her back close to him.

Kat Roberts revved her Harley Sportster and sped away from the Beauty Box. She wanted to put as much distance between her and Aunt Tammy as possible. She grinned at the locals' stares as she roared down the street.

She'd been transplanted from one family mess to another. This one wouldn't keep her down, though. Things were finally starting to go her way; she was free from her mother, on her own, and making a living in a nice place. Tammy wasn't going to drive her out of town. Kat tightened her grip on the motorcycle. No one and nothing would stand in the way of her happiness this time. She'd make sure of it.

Dina peered through the steam at the marinara sauce she was cooking. This was Tammy's favorite sauce. She sampled a spoonful. Delicious. She hoped Tammy would like it. Maybe things would start looking up again. Tammy had behaved badly at the Beauty Box today, but everyone was entitled to a bad day. She'd done a lot for Dina and she wouldn't give up on her friend.

She turned and smiled as Tammy walked in.

"Hi, Tammy," said Dina shyly, pushing back the frizzy lock of hair that fell in her eyes. Her glasses were foggy with the steam. She pushed the large frames up to the top of her small nose.

Tammy glanced at the sauce. "Count me out for supper, Dina."

Dina said unhappily, "Oh. I thought you were going to be around tonight. You've got plans?"

"Connor is picking me up. We're grabbing supper."

"Oh. Okay." There was a time when Tammy would have asked Dina to join them. But Tammy hadn't been herself for a while.

"Aren't you dyeing Kat's hair tonight?" asked Tammy. She didn't wait for Dina to answer, but opened the pantry door and glared at the contents. "I asked you to pick up some tonic water and limes at the store." She slammed the pantry closed.

Dina's long face fell even further. "I-I'm sorry, Tammy. I had the pasta ingredients on the brain and just forgot to go to the store." Tammy glared at her before stomping into the back. "I really am writing you out of my will, you know. You and Kat both. I don't need either one of you."

Dina took a deep breath and tried to steady her nerves. Tammy was getting worse. Everything was changing again, right when life was finally starting to look up.

Clover and wild onions flew through the air as Agnes Walker weeded her backyard flowerbed with a vengeance. She scowled at the impudent dandelions. Anxiety and anger made her forgo her hoe and lent her strength to yank up a small patch of crab grass with her bare hands. The afternoon heat finally took its toll. Agnes pulled off her wide-brimmed hat, fanning herself with it before giving up on gardening and going in for a tall glass of sweet tea.

She frowned at her phone. She'd call Connor, but wasn't sure she wanted to risk hearing him in a bad mood. He'd always been the perfect son, a great asset for an elderly widow. Dating Tammy was the one thing she'd fault him on.

Most girls weren't good enough for Connor. That girl he brought home from college, for instance. Agnes shuddered.

She'd risk it. Agnes picked up the phone and briskly dialed Connor's number. His harried voice finally answered. "Mother, what is it?"

"Nothing important, Connor. Just calling to see how things were going."

"I'm about to run out the door. Can I call you later?"

"It wasn't anything important." Agnes hesitated before asking, "Are you going out with Tammy tonight?"

Connor's voice now had an edge to it. "Yes, Mother. Look, I've got to go—"

"Of course, of course. Just. . .be careful."

Agnes softly placed the phone on the hook and sat for a long time staring at it.

Red's cell phone rang early the next morning as he was sitting at the kitchen table with his face half-submerged in a bowl of Cheerios. Red groaned.

"Hello?" he demanded in an early-morning scratchy voice. He listened intently for a moment. "I'll be right there." He strode to the bedroom, emerging a minute later wearing his uniform and a grim expression. Elaine gazed curiously at him as he grabbed his car keys off the counter. "Tammy Smith is dead. Her niece discovered her body at the Beauty Box this morning. It sounds like murder."

Chapter Four

It was nice to have a spy Myrtle could count on. And her neighbor, Miles, made an excellent spy. Somehow, when Myrtle looked pushy and nosy, Miles simply appeared innocuously observant. And when he asked questions, he was able to fly under Red's radar, which wasn't the case for Myrtle. So of course it was Miles she turned to when she needed a set of eyes over at the Beauty Box. Priority number one was to find out more about Tammy's mysterious death. Was it an accident? Or murder?

The only problem was that she'd forgotten about the painting she'd left on Miles' doorstep.

"Oh, it's you," said Miles. "I was just about to call you."

"About Tammy's death?"

"No, about the other atrocity...that painting you foisted on me. With the cryptic, *thinking of you*, message. I can only assume, looking at the painting, that message was meant as an insult."

Myrtle paused. "What if I told you that I'd painted that painting in honor of our friendship and our mutual love for books?"

"I wouldn't believe you. If you'd created something like that, you'd have put it out of its misery. You're too much of an aesthete to have unleashed something that ghastly on the world."

"An astute observation. No, I didn't paint it. But Elaine did. And she *loves* it and she thinks *I* love it and now she's going to think that *you* love it, too. It's supposed to be you and me, surrounded by books."

Miles' voice was dubious. "Are you sure? I thought it was some sort of market scene. There are so many people in it."

"No, no, you're looking at it wrong. Those aren't people; they're *books*."

"What? They couldn't be. Oh wait. I'm looking at the painting upside-down. I see the signature." There was some fumbling around on the other side of the phone. "And now it's even worse. I need you to take this back, Myrtle."

"For heaven's sake! It's not all that bad. Just keep it in your closet for a while until it's my turn to curate the blasted thing. And be sure to pull it out and put it on your mantel if Elaine comes by!" Miles started to argue, so Myrtle hurried on, "But you've distracted me. This isn't why I called. I wanted to talk to you about the murder at the Beauty Box. Are you up for a reconnaissance mission?"

"Can't you find out the scoop by yourself?" Miles sounded cranky.

"I would absolutely love to, Miles. Unfortunately, I'm too high-profile."

"What?"

"They'd know that I was prying. When people think you're being snoopy, they don't share information—they clam up. You'll just look haplessly oblivious, and those old biddies at the salon will be falling all over themselves to fill you in. Mark my words," said Myrtle.

Miles grouchily agreed to go.

And soon he was phoning back. It seemed like record time to Myrtle.

"I couldn't linger too long, you know. I was beginning to look a little suspicious, lurking around outside the Beauty Box," said Miles.

"Never mind the excuses, Miles. What *did* you see?"

"I saw that an unusual death in Bradley is still enough of a novelty to bring out all the onlookers. And that the local gossip mill is still in full swing. There's really no need for *The Bradley Bugle*. Everybody here gets the news just a few minutes after it happens."

"Did you find out anything *useful*, though?" said Myrtle, trying unsuccessfully to curb her impatience. "How did Tammy die? Was there any evidence pointing to anybody? Was it an accident or murder?"

Miles said, "I'm pretty sure it was murder. I saw the state police pull up and a forensic team with those spacesuit-looking things on. But I didn't get any real information—it was all just people gawking."

"That's not a whole lot of information, Miles." She was going to have to rethink Miles' usefulness as a sidekick if this was all her spy could come up with.

Miles' voice was exasperated. "Then why don't *you* head over there, Myrtle. Threaten to thump those police officers with your cane if they don't give you the scoop."

"I don't want to. It's got to be about two hundred degrees out there. Besides, I don't like rubbing shoulders with all those rubberneckers. No thanks. I bet I can make Red tell me what's going on later."

"Really?"

Myrtle bristled at the doubt in her friend's voice. "Absolutely! Just leave it to me."

"Traditionally you've had a tough time getting Red to tell you *anything*. Isn't he the same Red who nearly admitted you into a retirement home without your knowledge?"

"Forget all that, Miles. That's ancient history. Red and I have an *understanding* now. I'm sure he'll be happy to give me the scoop on the case. After all, I even wrote an investigative piece on the last murder for the paper."

"By the way, I've been meaning to ask you about book club. Are you reading this month's selection?"

Myrtle could swear she heard a hint of a snicker. It was not becoming. "I'm really not into stories where vampires and zombies duel it out. If I'm not mistaken, that's what the rest of our so-called book club is reading. No, Miles, this murder has put me in a Gothic frame of mind. I think Edgar Allan Poe is in order. I'll check in with you later."

Myrtle stepped into her living room and pulled out a battered collection of Poe's works ("a quaint and curious volume of forgotten lore...") from her living room shelf. She sank down onto her sofa and flipped to *The Raven*. Sleepy from a bout of insomnia the night before, she started drowsing off as she read.

A repetitive rapping disturbed her napping. Myrtle jerked awake and hurried to her front door. Miles might have forgotten to give her an important detail from his reconnaissance mission.

She pulled the door open without looking and kicked herself for it when she saw the rodent-like features of her next door neighbor, Erma Sherman. Myrtle stood solidly in the door to make sure Erma couldn't sneak by her and take over her living room. She was like the devil to get rid of.

"I thought I should do an elderly neighbor check," said Erma affecting a noble look. "Considering there's a deranged murderer around."

Myrtle gritted her teeth. "Thanks for your concern. As you can see, though, I'm just fine. So while I appreciate your worrying, Erma, it's misguided. And now, if you'll excuse me, I've got some laundry to wrangle." She turned, but for some reason tripped over her left foot and stumbled before catching herself with her cane.

She cursed under her breath as Erma quickly used her stumble as an opening and propelled both Myrtle and herself into the house, slamming the door shut behind her. "Here, Myrtle! Let me give you a hand. You should take it easy! How about a nice glass of warm milk while you put your feet up?"

Myrtle was about to tell Erma what she could do with her warm milk when she was interrupted by more incessant Erma chatter. "I hear that someone pushed Tammy down the stairs. Now who would do a thing like that?" Erma's lips parted in a grin. "Everyone, that's who! No one could stand her!"

"Did you get your hair done there, Erma?" It would be nice to get *some* sort of helpful information out of this invasion. Although there was no way that Tammy could have been responsible for the mess that was Erma Sherman's coiffure. Not even a completely-incapacitated-by-drink Tammy.

"Sometimes. But most of my information I got from other people—friends. Women talk, you know." Boy, do they. Especially the Erma variety of women.

There was a rap at the front door. "You're very popular today, aren't you?" brayed Erma. "*I'll* get the door, Myrtle! You just settle down in a chair."

Amazingly, it was Myrtle's housekeeper, Puddin, who saved the day. Puddin, who never showed up to clean Myrtle's house unless all the stars were lined up just right in the heavens. Puddin, whose back got thrown at the hint of dust or dirty floors. Puddin! There she was, at the door, with her usual sullen and suspicious face with Myrtle's cat, Pasha. Pasha, the feral black cat that Erma was horribly allergic to. Myrtle started to smile.

"Cat wants in," grunted Puddin around a cigarette, which she hastily removed from her mouth at Myrtle's glare. The cat streaked into the house and, with unerring instinct, launched itself at Erma.

"Cat! Cat!" squawked Erma, moving first one direction, then another, like an indecisive squirrel in the path of an oncoming car. "Let it out!"

"Cat wants in," stated Puddin, already slouching toward the kitchen to use Myrtle's own cleaning supplies.

"See you later!" yelled the fleeing Erma, already sneezing and leaving the front door open in her haste to leave.

"Not if I see you first," muttered Myrtle. She closed and locked the door, leaning back against it with relief. Pasha was an angel. An absolute angel cat sent from the heavens to reward Myrtle for some sort of unknown and unusual good behavior. Pasha rhythmically bathed herself in satisfaction. She was well-aware that she was a good girl.

"Puddin," called out Myrtle, "I'm shocked to see you. What's put you in the cleaning mood today? I was thinking this was going to be a two-or-three reminder week, for sure."

Puddin stuck her head through the living room door, watching Pasha. "Can't you put that cat away? It puts hexes on me."

"A ridiculous and harmful superstition about black cats that I'm sick of hearing about. She'll leave you alone if you leave her alone," Myrtle sat down on the sofa. "And I do suggest you leave her alone."

Puddin shrugged. "I'll leave soon, anyway. I went to clean the Beauty Box and the cops sent me away. Thought I'd get you out of the way since I'm here anyway." She resentfully slapped the dust off an end table and ignored the way it immediately resettled in the same spot.

"You were at the Beauty Box this morning? What was going on over there?" asked Myrtle.

Puddin, always looking for an opportunity to chat and forgo cleaning, plopped down next to Myrtle. She put her feet up on the coffee table and leaned back, looking at the ceiling as if her visit to the Beauty Box was replaying there in digital quality. "Kat was off to one side of the salon and she looked bad. Real sick!" said Puddin with some malevolence. "White as snow while she talked with the cops. Her hands shook and she borrowed a cigarette off me. That Dina, the quiet, skinny one, was crying in a corner of the shop."

"So you actually went *inside* then?"

"Course! Needed to clean, didn't I?" asked Puddin scornfully.

This expectation frequently didn't translate into an *actual* cleaning. Myrtle frowned back at Puddin. "Go on!"

Puddin basked in her sudden spotlight as storyteller. "Well, I heard Dina boo-hooing about what was she going to do now? Tammy was supposed to be the one putting her up. Now where's she going to live? Where's she going to work if the Beauty Box was to close? That sort of thing." Puddin waved her doughy hands in the air to signify additional, nebulous Dina concerns.

"Kat was upset, too? Shocked?" asked Myrtle.

Puddin scowled. "No. She looked tough as nails, like usual. You know what she's like. So she was lighting up the cigarette I gave her, looking kind of sick, telling the cops that she'd gone in early to get the towels from the washer to dry them for the customers. Tammy puts the towels in the washer at night and Kat puts them in the dryer in the morning. The washer and dryer are at the bottom of the stairs, down in the basement. Kat turns on the light to go down the stairs and there's Tammy at the bottom." Puddin nodded her head in emphasis.

Myrtle said, "Oh, okay. Those stairs are really steep, aren't they?"

"They're dreadful. Told them I wasn't doing their laundry nor doing their ironing, neither. Wasn't going down them."

That certainly sounded likely. "So Tammy, who was highly intoxicated when I saw her yesterday, took a drunken stumble down a steep set of stairs when she was trying to put a bunch of towels down there. Case closed. I guess the police had to investigate, anyway. Probably protocol."

Puddin was already shaking her head, looking smug. "It was murder. She had a pair of hair shears sticking out of her, too. Somebody done killed her, all right."

"Hair shears! Are you sure?"

"I heard Kat and the police talking about it. Scissors. Jabbed right into her back, then she was shoved. Dead as a doornail."

"And no real clues to the killer? No evidence or confessions or anything?"

Puddin shook her head. "Everybody wanted to kill her. She was blabbing secrets. But Kat probably killed her." Here the malevolent look again. Puddin didn't like people who were of more than average attractiveness. "For the money."

"Did Tammy *have* any money? It seems unlikely," said Myrtle.

"Had her own shop, didn't she?" Puddin raised her eyebrows to emphasize her point. "All those customers? Bet she had some money put away."

If she hadn't drunk most of it in the last few weeks.

"And she's tough, that Kat. Looks like a thug. Maybe she learned about killing up in New York," Puddin's eyes were big.

"I think she *looks* tough, but she's not as tough as she looks. Although I have to admit that with all her bodily embellishments, she bears a startling resemblance to Queequeg."

Puddin squinted at her.

"All right, Puddin, that's enough visiting. Might as well get your cleaning done, if you're here."

Puddin scowled. "Not too much, though. My back is thrown."

PUDDIN HAD DONE A SURPRISINGLY thorough job with the cleaning. She might have been so distracted thinking about the case that she accidentally did more cleaning than usual. She was even perspiring quite a bit by the time she left.

"Hot as the hinges in here," Puddin growled as she pushed her way out Myrtle's door.

"Hang on—those are mine!" Myrtle grabbed back her floor cleaner, ammonia, and furniture polish. "You never bring your cleaners, remember? And it's not all that hot in here."

"It is if you're not a hundred years old," said the vengeful Puddin as she kicked through the door.

"I've got *years* to go before I'm a hundred! Years!" hollered Myrtle behind her.

It pained her to admit that Puddin was right. It was a little on the warm side in her house. She irritably plopped onto her living room sofa and jumped in horror as she glimpsed her mantel. The painting! How had it gotten there? That Puddin! Miles must have paid her to sneak it into the house. Puddin was easily bribed.

Myrtle pushed herself up, grabbed the painting and shoved it under her sofa. Then she stomped off to take a look at her thermostat. Eighty-five degrees.

A call to the air conditioning repairman confirmed that they were backed up and couldn't get to her at least two more days.

It seemed like an excellent time to visit Miles. With a painting in tow.

Miles seemed less than excited to see her. "Actually, Myrtle, I was just about to head off to the gym. Didn't we just talk to each other?"

"Oh, the gym is open for hours. Can't you offer an old lady refuge from the heat?"

"You can't take refuge in your own house?" asked Miles, motioning her inside with a resigned look on his face.

"Unfortunately, my house is what I need refuge *from*. The air is broken. Naturally it only breaks down during the hottest part of the summer. They can't get to it for days, either. T.S. Eliot obviously never spent a summer in the South if he thought April was the cruelest month."

Miles raised his eyebrows. "It'll be a hundred degrees in your house! You aren't planning to stay there, are you? Or at least I can let you borrow some box fans I've got."

Myrtle carefully hid a smile. "Can't you let me stay with you? In your guest room?"

"Here?" Miles was flustered. "What would Erma Sherman say? She'd tell everyone we were living together! You've got to be joking."

"I am," said Myrtle, grinning. "But I have to say the way you *didn't* leap to offer me your guest room is discouraging. Never mind. I have my own plans. It's all about making lemonade out of lemons, you know. I'm going to stay with Red and Elaine. Gives me the perfect opportunity to grill Red about the murder."

"Here we go again," said Miles with an exaggerated sigh. "We don't even know it *is* a murder, Myrtle."

"Actually..." said Myrtle, "we do. Puddin came by today to clean for me. And it wasn't even her day," she added pointedly.

Miles seemed very busy fussing with his gym bag.

"She'd shown up at the Beauty Box to do her regular cleaning there and heard Kat talking to the police. Said Tammy was stabbed with some hair shears. It's murder, all right."

Miles looked a little more interested. "So tell me some of what was going on at your last appointment there. You said Tammy had been causing trouble."

"Unfortunately, it all involves a lot of guessing because Tammy wasn't clearly spelling everything out—just sort of making these wild innuendoes. But she said something about Bootsie Davenport's young man and it flustered Bootsie like crazy."

Miles sat down on the sofa, apparently accepting that the exercising would be put off a little longer. "Bootsie...this is Judge Davenport's wife. The society maven. At least, a society maven for Bradley, North Carolina."

"That's right. And she acted like Tammy was talking about their college-age son, but Tammy made it pretty clear she wasn't. She also said something about Prissy Daniels."

Miles snorted. "What could Tammy possibly have on Prissy Daniels? That she drives two miles over the speed limit? That she doesn't play piano as well as she claims? She's a Sunday school teacher, for heaven's sake."

"And a preschool director," reminded Myrtle. "But that doesn't mean that she doesn't have a secret life." Just the words alone gave Myrtle a thrill. She loved uncovering secrets. Particularly from goody-goodies like Prissy. "Tammy was real vague again, as far as her gossip went. Said something about us not knowing the *real* Prissy. It sure got a reaction out of Prissy. She must have known something."

"So, Bootsie and Prissy. Anybody else get smeared during their weekly pilgrimage to the Beauty Box? I'm starting to be glad I go to the barber. Bill just cuts my hair. He hums sometimes, but that's it."

"It sounds dead boring to me," said Myrtle with a sniff. "At least the Beauty Box has entertainment included in the price of services. Let's see. Tammy was ugly to Kat because Kat was obviously completely embarrassed by the way her aunt was acting. So she sort of insulted her. And, of course, the brilliant Puddin thought that Kat might have a financial motive."

"That's just naturally the type of angle that Puddin would consider, though. She's in challenging financial circumstances, after all," said Miles, sounding reproachful.

"Only because her back gets thrown at the thought of work! Much as I hate to admit it, though, Puddin might possibly have something. Kat *would* get the shop and Tammy probably had a little bit put away somewhere. And she wouldn't have to be bossed around by anybody—money would bring her some independence, which is probably what she wants most. She's had no control over her future, and money would give her a little security."

Miles pushed his glasses up his nose, a reflexive motion when he was thinking. "Wasn't there somebody else who lived there with Tammy, too?"

"Ohhh yes. Dina. She's Tammy's project, back from when Tammy was sober enough to take on projects. She was escaping a bad marriage, and Tammy took her in and gave her a job. But she was acting ugly to Dina yesterday, too."

"Maybe Dina got fed up with it?" said Miles. "The final straw kind of thing? Maybe she snapped?"

Myrtle considered this. "*Maybe.* I hear her husband was abusive, so it could be that Tammy triggered some pent-up anger. I don't know, though—I just can't see it. Although Tammy *was* threatening to write

Dina and Kat out of her will. That could have provided motive enough to kill her—before she could make any changes."

Myrtle pushed herself off the sofa. "Okay! You can go to the gym now, Miles. I just wanted to give you the low-down. We've got another case to solve."

"Don't you mean *you* do?" asked Miles dryly. "As I recall, you like to be in charge of your cases."

"Yes, but sleuths need sidekicks, Miles. Sounding boards. Sherlock had Watson, Poirot had Hastings. And I have you. But sidekicks do their best work in the background, you know. They're the behind the scenes guys." Myrtle watched him carefully for signs of insurrection, but saw nothing in his placid expression. She smiled.

"And now it really *is* time for me to go to the gym," said Miles, standing up and motioning to Myrtle.

"Of course. But could you give me a glass of water real quick, Miles? My house was warmer than I realized. I'm feeling pretty dry."

As he slipped into the kitchen, she reached out Miles' front door and grabbed the shopping bag she'd left there. The painting was settled nicely behind an armchair before he got back with the water.

Chapter Five

"**A**re you *sure* Mama's air conditioner isn't working?" Red asked. "Why do I feel like this is some mastermind plot to squeeze information about this murder out of me?"

"Well, I couldn't exactly ask your mother for proof." said Elaine. "She told me the air was broken and that the guy wouldn't be able to come out for a couple of days. July isn't the best month to live in an un-air conditioned house in the deep South."

Red rubbed his eyes. "I just hope she won't start being nosy. You know how she is. Always putting herself in the middle of the action."

"She's only trying to stay cool, Red. You should give your mom the benefit of the doubt. Besides, would it really hurt to give her just a couple of minor details about the murder?"

"Elaine, you know I can't do that."

"Would it really matter that much? You could just give her something to think about. Not everything with the case is top secret, is it? You know how she loves to try to puzzle out these mysteries. And she's not the only one. The whole town of Bradley is curious, Red. Think of the throngs in the street."

"Throngs? In Bradley? I haven't seen them, but even if they exist, they're not playing detective—they're just looking for gossip. I saw that gleam in Mama's eye. In that twisted mind of hers, she's clutching a magnifying glass, smoking a pipe, and wearing a deer-stalker cap."

Elaine said, "She could actually help you out. She's solved cases before."

"Endangering her life in the process."

"She's an old lady, Red, and I think she's slowing down a little. This time she might be a Nero Wolfe and solve the case from home."

"Maybe she'll be a Miss Marple type who sticks her nose in where it doesn't belong."

"Maybe you could just share some minor case trivia with her tonight."

"Maybe I could nip her nosiness in the bud tonight."

Elaine turned and looked meaningfully into his eyes. "Yard gnomes, Red. With red hats. Dozens of them."

Red shuddered. Arguments with his mother were followed by Myrtle dragging out her collection of ceramic garden gnomes and placing them all over her front yard. The coy gnomes (and his neighbors) stared at him accusingly until Myrtle got her way. And she always, always got her way.

"All right. I'll give her some sort of briefing. But I might give her red herrings instead of clues."

Myrtle's doorbell rang and this time she carefully peeped out the door to make sure it wasn't Erma Sherman. She opened it when she saw Red. "What a lovely habit this is starting to be, Red! Two visits in two days."

Red grunted something as he walked in, then stopped. "Wow. It's hot in here."

"Exactly what I told Elaine," said Myrtle primly. Red clearly thought she'd come up with some sort of trumped up excuse to stay with them. She watched as he stomped his way to her back hall. "And the thermostat is set to seventy," she said complacently.

"Well, I can't say I'm shocked. It's about time for something like this to happen. I've said for a long time that this house needs some repairs done. That's another great thing about living in a retirement community, Mama. You don't have to worry about home repairs anymore. If you've got a busted pipe or a bunch of electrical problems, the retirement home folks are the ones who have to foot the bill."

Myrtle deftly ignored the last part. "I don't know what you mean about the house needing work. It's running just fine. The air conditioner probably just needs Freon or something."

"Well, looking around, I already see a bunch of stuff that could be done. These scatter rugs are a menace for one thing. You could break your neck on those. It sounds to me like one of your toilets is running...that's got to be costing you every month." He swung his head around and frowned, looking toward the ceiling. "Where are your smoke detectors? And carbon monoxide detectors?"

"My smoke detector is right there, Red. Over the front door. I only need one. This house is about as big as a breadbox."

Red strode across the living room in a couple of steps. "This?" He pressed a test button on the smoke detector and there was a spectacular silence in response. Myrtle cursed under her breath. They didn't make batteries like they used to; she was sure of it.

"Now this is alarming, Mama," said Red, putting his hands on his hips.

"No pun intended?" she asked smoothly.

"I'm going to install some smoke detectors for you. You should have one in the kitchen, one in the bedroom, one near your garage. With functioning batteries."

"*You* don't need to do anything, Red! I'm fully capable of taking care of this myself. And I will—the very next time I go to the store. I had no idea the batteries were dead in that thing. I think having three or four smoke detectors is overkill, but all right."

Red stomped off toward the bedroom, probably looking for more safety infractions. "Got a suitcase packed?" he called.

"Right there inside my bedroom door. And I've got a grocery bag of food to bring over with me."

Red joined her with the suitcase. "Now that's something you *don't* have to worry about. Elaine and I can afford to feed an extra mouth, you know."

"Just the same, I don't want to be any bother," Myrtle said righteously.

Red seemed to be biting his tongue. He grabbed the bag of food and he and Myrtle walked across the street. Myrtle leaned feebly on her cane. "You just don't know how much I appreciate this, Red, especially considering how you're so busy right now. You don't have a whole lot of time for houseguests, what with a murder on your hands." Would he actually admit that it was murder?

"Well, it will mainly be Elaine who has to deal with you, Mama. I mean, Elaine who'll be making you feel at home. Murders sure don't happen every day in Bradley. You're right about being busy. I'm guessing I won't be at home much while you're visiting." He looked positively determined.

So Puddin was right. It was murder.

TWO O'CLOCK IN THE morning was a rough time of day if you were someone's insomniac houseguest.

You can't sleep. But you can't really get up and wake the whole house.

For a while Myrtle resigned herself to contemplating the guest room ceiling. If she were at home, she'd get up and be productive—put away the pots and pans she'd put in the sink to soak, fold some clean laundry, pay a couple of bills. Or do a few crossword puzzles. But here she had a feeling she'd just bang into things and wake Jack up. Everybody knows the rule—you don't wake sleeping toddlers. Ever.

The other thing she'd do, if she were home, was go on a walk. Naturally, she'd end up at Miles' house. Miles was an insomniac too, bless him, and she'd almost always see a light on and go over and knock on his door. They'd have a cup of tea or a glass of wine, then Myrtle would walk back home and sleep soundly the rest of the night. The longer she contemplated the guest room ceiling, the better this plan seemed. She could talk with Miles some more about the case, too.

Myrtle pulled on her long robe, grabbed her cane, and conscientiously locked the door behind her with her copy of their house key. She set off down the silent street.

There was a little moon to light her way as she walked. And, sure enough, there was a light on in Miles' front window. They really formed a mini insomniacs support group.

Myrtle rapped on Miles' door and he immediately opened it. He wore a long, navy blue bathrobe belted tightly over what looked like plaid pajamas. "Want some tea?" he asked, heading to his kitchen, slippers flopping as he walked. He looked completely unsurprised and started pulling out the measuring cup he used to boil water in.

"Did you even look out the peephole before you opened the door? Because there's a killer out there, remember?" Myrtle followed him into his kitchen and pulled out two teacups.

"No, of course I didn't look. It's two o'clock in the morning, Myrtle. Who else visits me this time of day? At least I was awake this time. I don't *always* have a hard time sleeping, you know. Are we really convinced there *is* a killer? Do killers knock on doors, anyway?"

"I'm sure they would if they knew that you'd just open the door right up. Never mind. I woke up, couldn't go back to sleep, started thinking about the case, and decided to visit. Oh. And I decided to assign you a mission, since you're all gung-ho about being a sidekick."

Maybe gung-ho was the wrong word. Miles was looking decidedly apprehensive.

He pushed his glasses up his nose. "What kind of mission? I'm not going to be able to fly under Red's radar as much if we overdo my snooping around."

Myrtle waved her hand dismissively. "Where you're going wrong with your information-gathering technique is that you're passing it off like idle gossip or being snoopy. What *you* do well is polite concern."

"Polite concern."

"Yes. You don't want to be *involved* with the problem, but you're politely providing an ear for the poor person who is in need of getting something off her chest. That's your angle," said Myrtle.

The microwave bleated, announcing that the water was heated. Myrtle put tea bags in their cups and Miles covered them with hot water. "And whom am I supposed to be directing this polite concern toward?"

"That's what I was mulling over. I'm leaning toward Dina. She's absolutely pitiful, and she'd be a natural choice for you to be sympathetic to. She might be the only person around who still *liked* Tammy. And, after all, she was her housemate. Maybe she saw or heard something on the night of the murder. I mean, really, can someone be the victim of a violent crime and fall down a staircase and *not* be heard? Tammy wasn't a small woman."

Miles took a sip of his tea and winced at the hot water. "You have a point. We should find out what Dina was doing when Tammy was murdered. Actually, we should find out when Tammy was murdered, period. Got any ideas on finding out the time of death? It'll be hard to figure out if alibis are genuine unless we know the estimated time of death."

"You're starting to sound like one of those forensic crime shows, Miles."

"It's the truth! And, considering where you're staying, it seems to make more sense for you to be the one to find out when Tammy died. I'm sure Red knows. Maybe even Elaine knows, if Red is in the habit of talking with her about cases."

"All right. I guess I'll do the dirty work, then. And you go see Dina and pat her on the back for a while."

A loud knock on Miles' front door made both of them jump. "Better look through that peephole this time," murmured Myrtle. "Considering that it's definitely not me out there."

Miles cautiously looked out. "It's Red." he said as Myrtle cursed.

"Evening, Miles," said Red, courteous as usual to the older man. "Do you, by any chance, have my deranged mother over here for a visit?" Then he looked at Myrtle and shook his head. "I *thought* I should probably do a bed-check on you, so I set an alarm. Sure enough, you weren't in your room when I checked. Aren't you a little old to be sneaking out in the middle of the night?"

Myrtle tried to look as dignified as an octogenarian in a bathrobe could possibly pull off. "I was trying to spare y'all, that's all. I didn't want to wake up the whole house with my insomnia. Especially Jack. He gets up early enough as it is...a two a.m. wake up call was a little too much."

"He sure does get up early." Red looked sleepy just thinking about it.

"Tell you what—since I'm disturbing your sleep and probably Elaine's too, how about if I go on Jack-duty later this morning? When he wakes up, he can spend some quality time with his Nana." Myrtle felt pleased with herself. It was nice to Do Good. Traces of an old hymn floated through her brain.

Red rubbed his temples. "I suppose so, Mama. But can you just come back home with me and stop imposing on Miles? I can't sleep until I know you're safely back in bed."

Myrtle blinked at him. "I can't imagine why you're so concerned, Red. After all, Tammy's killer acted first thing in the morning before the Beauty Box opened. He's probably conked out somewhere, fast asleep and dreaming evil thoughts...not out attacking little old ladies in the middle of the night."

"Where did you get the idea that she was killed in the morning? No, she was murdered sometime the night before. So it's *not* safe to be traipsing around Bradley, North Carolina, in your PJs." Red strode to Miles' door, and Myrtle turned and gave Miles a long wink. Apparently the key to weaseling information from Red was to trick it out of him in the wee hours of the morning.

HAPPY TODDLER TALK woke Myrtle at six o'clock. She pulled on bright blue knit pants and a knit top and peered into Jack's room. He stood on his bed, watching Myrtle suspiciously. It was nearly dawn, the only time of day for a walk when the weather was scorching. "Mama?" he asked.

"Oh, we don't need Mama right now, Mr. Jack. We're going to have ourselves a happy walk."

Jack, still eyeing Myrtle with puzzlement, clutched his lovey, Dirty Doggy, in a chubby hand. Dirty Doggy's filth had reached epic proportions and Jack's attachment showed no signs of easing up. This morning Dirty Doggy was sporting the evidence of Jack's dinner last night. According to Dirty Doggy's coat, Jack had feasted on pureed peas and had, as usual, insisted on his friend's presence with him as he ate.

Dirty Doggy was in dire need of a day at the spa. The stroller ride would distract Jack from missing his friend, and the wash cycle would be over when they got back. If Jack got too desperate, she could always hand it over, still soggy. Myrtle grabbed the offending item and marched to the laundry room. After dumping in half a container of soap and stain-remover, she hurried back to Jack.

"Nana's fixing you some breakfast, sweetie," said Myrtle. Jack opened his small mouth to protest. "Uh-uh," said Myrtle in her best no-nonsense tone. "We're letting Mama sleep."

What did little guys eat for breakfast? She felt Jack's eyes boring critically into her as she fumbled around in the pantry. Myrtle surveyed the dazzling display of chips and breakfast cereal in Elaine's pantry while Jack muttered under his breath.

"Let's eat and run, sweetie," said Myrtle, making an executive decision. She grabbed a banana, put some cereal in a zipper bag, and headed to the garage with Jack.

Jack climbed into the umbrella stroller and Myrtle absently offered him the banana. Would Agnes be up this early? Probably. Shouldn't she have seen or heard something? Her house was right next door to the Beauty Box. If the murder had taken place some point before midnight, then Agnes would have probably been awake. She was a night owl, for sure.

The sound of her name stopped her. Agnes Walker's expression suggested that she'd called her name a few times already. "Time to invest in hearing aids, Myrtle?"

Myrtle had *excellent* hearing. "I'm just thinking, that's all."

"Are you *sure* you're thinking this morning? Poor Jack might be trying to get your attention, too. A whole banana? Couldn't you have at least peeled the thing? Poor child. Let's go inside so Miss Agnes can take care of you." Agnes stuck her newspaper under her arm, took Jack by his hand and helped him out of the stroller. He trotted beside her into the house.

Myrtle was feeling a little sour, but bit her tongue. She needed to get information from Agnes, after all. She parked the stroller outside the front door and followed Agnes in.

Myrtle winced at the baby talk that Agnes was speaking to Jack. There was something unattractive about baby talk coming out of a seventy-year-old face. Besides, Jack was way past baby talk. He could even speak some Spanish and French for heaven's sake. How had Connor turned out so well? You'd think he'd still be calling bananas *nanners*, if that was how Agnes had talked to him. Agnes peeled the offending banana and was carefully slicing it up in small pieces on a china plate. Jack clapped his hands.

Myrtle said, impatiently, "So, what do you think happened to Tammy?" At Agnes' uncomprehending frown, she elaborated. "Who did her in, Agnes? It wasn't an accident, you know."

Agnes frowned. "Where are my manners this morning? Would you like a Coca-Cola or a coffee, Myrtle?"

Myrtle, realizing gossip wouldn't commence until all the pleasantries had been observed, agreed a Coke would be wonderful. When Agnes had given her the drink and a small napkin and once again addressed Jack with sickening baby talk, she sat down facing Myrtle.

"Maybe it was a drifter?" asked Agnes.

"I doubt there are vicious vagrants roaming Bradley. This was somebody Tammy knew. I'm sure of it."

Agnes fiddled with her glass, swirling the ice cubes around and staring at the fizz. "We're not supposed to speak ill of the dead, but we all wanted to kill her, after her performance at the salon. You know that."

"She didn't direct any barbs at me," said Myrtle, somewhat indignant over Tammy's discrimination against her. She absently watched Jack squeeze the banana through his fingers.

"She didn't say anything directly against me, either, but got my back up teasing me about Connor." Agnes' face turned a spotty red with the memory. Myrtle wondered if Agnes took anything for high blood pressure.

"Did you see anything? You've got VIP seats at the Beauty Box, living right next door."

"I didn't see or hear a thing. I spent the evening reading."

"The whole evening? It must have been a really absorbing book. What was the name of it?"

Agnes said with irritation, "I can't remember anything these days. Some political thriller or other."

That wasn't likely. Agnes had a penchant for weighty biographies and a mind like a steel trap. Jack was now smearing the remains of the banana onto his arm. Figuring his finger painting would keep him occupied, Myrtle ignored it and changed tactics with Agnes. "Were Tammy and Connor happy together?"

Agnes gave a gloomy sigh. "They seemed to be. They were always going out to supper or to the movies. If Tammy was acting like her old self, I swear I wouldn't have minded them dating. Drinking brought out the worst in her, though. I hated seeing the two of them together. To be perfectly honest," Agnes said with a hard edge to her voice, "I'm not sorry she's dead."

Agnes finally noticed that Jack's arm had a little banana sculpture on it and that he was now experimenting with banana as a hair conditioner. Clicking her tongue, she strode to the kitchen for some paper towels. She looked vigorous. Agnes was her friend, but she was certainly strong enough to plunge some scissors into someone's back and push her down the stairs. Could she possibly have killed Tammy to keep her away from Connor? Myrtle wondered if *any* woman was good enough for Agnes' Connor.

While Agnes used most of a paper towel roll to clean Jack up, Myrtle asked, "What was Tammy getting at with poor Prissy? And with Bootsie Davenport?"

Agnes shook her gray head. "She obviously thinks Bootsie is running around on her husband. Whether she knew something definite or not, I don't know. Maybe Tammy saw Bootsie out with some man. Or maybe Bootsie told Tammy during Tammy's more discreet days. But Prissy Daniels? I can't imagine getting any dirt on her. She seems completely innocuous."

Myrtle frowned. "Tammy might have been inventing trouble. She was picking at everybody else there, too. She sure made it hard to pin the murder on one person. I guess the main suspects must be Kat, Bootsie, Prissy, and Dina."

Agnes said, "And probably me." At Myrtle's raised eyebrows, she added, "Oh, don't act so innocent. You know I didn't want Connor to date Tammy. I've been pretty open about that." Agnes set down the almost empty roll of paper towels and gazed absently at the cleaner and shinier Jack.

"What about Bo? I remember hearing Tammy trash-talking him, saying how he mistreated her. I know their marriage ended badly."

Agnes gave an unladylike snort. "*She* bullied *him*, you mean. Bo is too much a gentleman to talk ugly about a lady, so the slander remains."

Jack, bored with the genteel and unchanging scenery offered by Agnes' house, made a warning whine, so Myrtle cut the visit short. As she left, she couldn't shake the feeling that Agnes knew more than she was letting on.

THE COKE HAD PUT A little zip in Myrtle's step as she headed to the crime scene. Red's car was parked in front of the Beauty Box. And she thought she'd been saving Red from getting up too early. His middle of the night walk to Miles' house couldn't have messed up his sleep that badly. Myrtle leaned over the stroller. "Want to visit Daddy, Jack?" Jack crowed, "Daddy!" "He'll love a visit," said Myrtle in a convincing voice as she pushed the stroller to the shop entrance and under the police tape.

Red stared morosely at the back wall while slumping in one of the vinyl drying chairs. He leaped up, an angry flush creeping up his neck as he caught sight of his mother lifting up the police tape and pushing the stroller under it. "Mama! What the—? "

"Temper, temper. And watch your language in front of my grandson."

"Didn't you see the police tape stretched across the door? Are you having trouble with your eyesight?"

"Not as much as you are," she snapped, nodding pointedly at the drugstore reading specs in Red's hand. "I know you don't want anybody trampling in and messing up the crime scene, but it appears Forensics has finished making the rounds," she noted, surveying the fingerprint dust piled on every flat surface.

The Beauty Box looked the same as it always had. She tried to see the familiar room with new eyes. No clues jumped out at her, no oddly-placed objects. There were the same hair sprays, the same combs and scissors. It looked like it was frozen in time with one workstation set up with applicator bottles and latex gloves for a hair dye that hadn't yet occurred for a client that was very late.

Red said, "Yeah, the state police from the CCPS got over here yesterday morning and finished taking all their pictures and measurements. I suppose it's time to remove the tape." Jack was telling Red about the banana and reaching up with both arms to him. His father picked him up and regarded him absently as if wondering where he came from.

"Did the North Carolina State Police find anything out? Is Detective Perkins helping again?" asked Myrtle.

"He's the one assigned to the case. They'll have to get back to me on the forensic stuff."

"Did Tammy's face give any clues?" Myrtle asked.

Red stared at her uncomprehendingly.

"I mean, was it frozen in a grotesque mask or anything? Did she look surprised or angry?"

"Why yes, Mama, according to her contorted lips, she was obviously breathing the name of her killer. We're bringing in a lip-reader to tell us who the murderer was." Red rolled his eyes. "Of course not! Dead faces are dead faces. All I saw was a sloppy middle-aged woman who dressed oddly because she was drunk when she got ready to go out."

"Poor Tammy."

Red snorted. "Poor Tammy, nothing. The ugly truth is she'd riled up half the town. It's a wonder she wasn't killed sooner."

"That may be true but it doesn't justify murder. I'm surprised at you, Red! And you an officer of the peace."

Jack grabbed Red's keys and started playing with them. "I'm just saying she was the one who put herself in that position. Perkins and I have started making the rounds with interviews, and I can't believe some of the stuff I'm hearing about Tammy."

"Who are y'all interviewing?"

"We're..." Red paused and peered sideways at his mother. "You know I can't be discussing police business with you."

"You know you feel better when you can talk about it. It might even help give you some insights. And who better to talk things over with than your own mama?" Pulling on the old heartstrings never hurt.

Red was opening his mouth to argue, then snapped it shut again. Probably remembering her gnomes. She hid a smile at the thought of the barefoot, inanely grinning, accordion-playing gnome that she liked to position nearest to Red's house. "We're really just focusing on what happened in the days leading up to Tammy's death. Who she upset, what she did. Actually, they're probably going to want to talk to you, Mama, since you were getting beautified that day."

Myrtle frowned.

"No, you're not a suspect. Anyone who was at the Beauty Box Tuesday will have to be questioned. They know Tammy didn't talk dirt about you, but you witnessed her scene in the shop."

"So they're not really interviewing any of her other clients?"

"It looks like a crime committed in the heat of the moment. Like Tammy made somebody mad on Tuesday and they came back and killed her with the closest weapon on hand. The only weird thing is that the weapon was a brand-new pair of hair shears with no fingerprints on them and no evidence they were wiped down. The killer must have worn gloves, which doesn't jive with the spontaneity of the murder. But, yes, to answer your question, chances are it was someone she knew. She trusted the murderer enough to turn her back on him or her to go down the stairs to the laundry room."

Myrtle said slowly, "So y'all are probably talking to Bootsie Davenport, Prissy Daniels, and maybe Agnes Walker, too."

Red put Jack back into the stroller. "According to the witnesses, Tammy didn't really say anything negative about Mrs. Walker, but since Mrs. Walker was known to be upset that Tammy was dating her son, she's a suspect, too. Although I can't imagine she had anything at all to do with this murder. I'd be shocked. In my mind, I've ruled her out."

"I guess you're also interviewing the girls she worked with. Tammy was goading Kat while I was there and was being snide to Dina, too. Plus, she said something about cutting Kat and Dina out of her will. Were they really in her will?"

Red shook his head. "We haven't gotten that far yet. Who knows? Dina is still saying how Tammy helped her out when she had nowhere to go. But that still doesn't mean she couldn't have gotten mad at Tammy. Everybody else was mad at her, and they were only with her for short periods of time. Dina actually *lived* with Tammy."

Myrtle said, "And maybe Dina was in Tammy's will, and Dina decided she needed some money."

"It'll all come out in the interviews, I'm sure." Red frowned at his mother. "You're not trying to get involved in my case, are you? Sticking your nose in everywhere and bungling up the police work? You're no Miss Marple."

"Oh, no, Red. I'm way too young to be Miss Marple. I'd be Nancy Drew." Red didn't laugh. Myrtle said, "It's just that I'm planning on writing an article for the paper about the case. Sloan Jones loves my investigative pieces."

Red still squinted suspiciously at her. Jack tired of the keys and discovered his father's nose, yanking it with both fists, and causing tears to well up in Red's eyes until he pulled free.

"Just a reminder, Mama, someone in Bradley has killed once and could do it again. Checking your bingo cards for B-5 is safer than asking questions and trying to do my job for me." He let out a deep breath, then said in a seemingly careless way, "Find out if you're on Jink's Heating and Air's schedule, yet?" Myrtle glared at him and Red shrugged. "Just asking," he said.

When Myrtle and Jack walked in, a showered, dressed and made-up Elaine was busily cooking enough food to feed everyone on the street. She looked a lot more refreshed. The short break must have done her good. "There you are!" she smiled at Myrtle. She put down the spatula and pulled Jack into her arms for a hug. "Did you have a big adventure, Jack?" Elaine squeezed Myrtle's hand. "Thanks for getting up with Jack this morning, Myrtle.

A few minutes of extra sleep and a long shower have given me a new lease on life."

Elaine gave Jack a squeeze before he trotted off to his room. "He even looks a little sleepy. I think he's even ready for a morning nap! I'll just grab Dirty Doggy ..." she stopped at the stricken look on Myrtle's face. "I *won't* grab Dirty Doggy?"

"Thirty minutes on high heat should dry Dirty Doggy out," Myrtle answered, apologetically. She hurried to the dryer.

Chapter Six

T ammy was buried on a scorching Sunday afternoon. Dogs, hoping for stray breezes, lay very still under oak trees. Heat rose in squiggly waves from the asphalt. Kids who'd played catch the flag and red rover now spent all their time drifting in large black, blazing-hot inner tubes on the warm lake water. Temperatures flirted with 100 degrees by eleven that morning. Tammy's service was graveside, and a fair-sized crowd had turned out. "They probably want proof she's really dead," hissed Myrtle to Elaine.

Law enforcement, represented by Red and what appeared to be several officers from the state police, were also in attendance, hanging back and scrutinizing the mourners. They were probably hoping the murderer, overcome with remorse, would fling himself prostrate on the coffin, begging the victim for forgiveness. Or, at the very least, that they might spot a guilty face in the crowd.

Myrtle wondered where all the overcast Hollywood movie funerals were set. North Carolina services were fiendishly uncomfortable affairs featuring small graveside tents where the grieving family sat in shaded discomfort. Friends and lesser mourning relatives hovered in sweaty misery on the fringe of the oasis, hoping for a pastor with a succinct style.

Tammy's shortage of close family changed the protocol. Kat sat in the front row with an uneasy Dina next to her. With no other family or close friends to offend, the other mourners claimed seats on a first-come-first-served basis as they arrived.

. Dina started crying before the service had even really started. Tammy's ex-husband Bo, sitting behind Dina, leaned forward to pat her awkwardly on the back. Dina made a flustered attempt to ignore him, probably loyally remembering his alleged mistreatment of Tammy.

The preacher, whose pews Tammy hadn't darkened for several years, performed a standard service. Those in attendance appeared remarkably unaffected, with the exception of Dina and Bo, who were both crying, Dina with gulping sobs and Bo with loud sniffs accompanied by louder nose blowing. Bo reached forward and gave Dina a fresh tissue. She gratefully took it after a moment of hesitation.

Myrtle was just glad they'd finally made it to the funeral. Elaine and she'd arrived later than planned because Jack had picked their departure as an opportunity to knock over Red's cologne, which spilled all over his front and then onto Elaine. She hurried to change them both, flinging clothes off and throwing them on the den floor as she ran. Then she'd packed a bag for Jack to have at the babysitter's house. With a couple of rifles and some MREs, Jack could have fit in with, or possibly led, a survivalist group. For the most part, Myrtle had been able to stifle her sighs. Although Elaine drove to the funeral home at speeds that Myrtle found NASCAResque, they were the last to arrive at the funeral home and took up the rear of the procession. They stood in intense sunshine at the graveside.

Myrtle lost her balance while fanning herself with her program and stumbled. A hand grabbed her elbow and she looked up into Connor Walker's concerned face. The perfect moment for a private chat. She acted especially feeble, and Connor gently pulled Myrtle away to a stone bench located closer to the parked cars. Agnes glared helplessly at her from the crowd around the graveside. Probably contemplating faking a fit, too. Agnes clearly wasn't pleased by the tête-à-tête.

Myrtle plopped on the bench, and Connor whipped out a pristine monogrammed handkerchief. Myrtle attributed the cotton anachronism to the Agnes Effect. She dabbed her face politely, although she—like most very elderly people—didn't really perspire. "Heat getting to you, Miss Myrtle?" asked Connor. "I can't imagine you're overwhelmed by grief."

"No, Tammy and I only had a professional relationship. Not like yours," she said, peering up at him from the corners of her eyes.

Connor's attractive features clouded up. He was one of the lucky ones who'd won the genetic jackpot in the looks lottery. Jet-black hair with contrasting blue eyes, movie star jaw and perfect teeth. He dressed neatly and fashionably and never had a hair out of place. He was completely conscious of his attractive appearance, which should have detracted from it, but didn't.

"Actually, Miss Myrtle, our relationship was over—on my end, anyway. I ended our relationship while we were at a restaurant, thinking she wouldn't make a scene. But being out in public sure didn't stop her from pitching a fit."

"Excuse an old lady's nosiness, Connor, but what made you decide to break up with Tammy?"

"The fact she drank bourbon for breakfast didn't help. Tammy used to be a lot of fun. Pretty, smart, wicked sense of humor. But she was a mean drunk. And she drank all the time the last couple of months of her life."

"Too bad you had to go through all that."

"You mean that I'm *going* through all that," he said. "Now it looks like I'm a prime suspect. Tammy and I argued in public, we'd had a relationship, and I don't have an alibi."

"What *were* you doing that night?" asked Myrtle.

He stared at her oddly and opened his mouth to answer when Agnes materialized and shut him up. The service was over, and the assembled mourners sped to their cars where air conditioners were immediately turned to "Arctic" setting. The minister, wilting in his heavy black robes, watched wistfully as his short-term flock galloped away.

Elaine hurried to join Myrtle, Connor, and Agnes. "Are you all right, Myrtle?"

Agnes fixed her with a piercing stare, and Myrtle played a frail old lady again, realizing it wasn't much of a stretch. "I'm all right now that I'm sitting down. Thanks, Connor," she said, patting his leg. "The heat made me ill for a minute. Nauseated," she drawled to a sympathetic Elaine.

"Let's get in the car and blast the air," Elaine said and took Myrtle by the arm to help her up. Myrtle noticed Connor watch the sunlight blaze on Kat's cotton-candy hair as she walked to her Harley. At least Kat thought to wear black to the funeral. It was black *leather*, but still. Kat grinned up at Connor as they talked together for a few minutes. Agnes pursed her lips as she looked on.

Detective Lieutenant John Perkins walked up to Myrtle. "Hi, Mrs. Clover. Good to see you again."

If Perkins was at all concerned that he was dealing with Red's mother again with a murder investigation, he didn't show it. He also didn't seem to be dripping with sweat the way that Red was. As always, he looked cool and collected with super-short, iron gray hair that looked like the casualty of a military barber's clippers.

"Good to see you too, Detective Perkins. Red told me you might want to ask me some questions about Tammy and her last day at the Beauty Box."

"I'll plan on running by later today, Mrs. Clover, if you're planning to be around. Red told me that you were staying with him temporarily."

He'd likely put a lot of emphasis on that *temporarily*. "I'll be around." She was just opening her mouth to ask a couple of questions of her own when Perkins gave a stiff nod and walked abruptly off and back to Red. Myrtle sighed. Lt. Perkins was going to be as unhelpful as Red was.

Elaine helped Myrtle into the car and they drove to the sitter's house. Elaine heaved a sigh. "I guess we've done our good deed for the day, paying our respects to Tammy."

"'Paying our respects' is a stretch, since we didn't respect the new, unimproved Tammy."

"We paid them to the old Tammy, I guess," said Elaine. "The sober one who kept secrets. She hesitated for a moment before adding, "I guess you didn't find out too much from Connor. I heard some gossip about Connor and Bootsie having a fling."

Myrtle's eyes opened wide. "Connor and *Bootsie*? Is Bootsie having a midlife crisis? Rapping ringtones, complaints about her matronly hairdo. Affairs with younger men?"

"It's just talk and probably not even true. You know how Bradley gossip is."

"But if it's true, then it could mean more trouble for Connor. Maybe Tammy wasn't letting their relationship end, and he really wanted to be with Bootsie. Maybe Bootsie and Connor planned to get Tammy out of the way."

Elaine had stopped listening. Now that she had the funeral checked off her mental to-do list and relegated to an event of the distant past, she moved on to more current concerns. "I hope Jack was okay at the sitter's. He hasn't wanted to take a nap lately, but then when he *doesn't* take a nap, he gets really destructive..."

Myrtle ignored the fretting. She couldn't shake a feeling of foreboding. "You know, Elaine," she said, interrupting Elaine's monologue, "I don't think Tammy's spirit is resting peacefully. Her killer needs to be brought to justice before her soul can be at peace."

Elaine raised her eyebrows. "It's not like you to be fanciful."

It wasn't. "Maybe I'm being haunted by the ghost of Tammy Past. And she wants me to put her killer away so she can kick back and enjoy heaven a little."

"Could you leave your friendly ghost over at your own house? I don't think I can handle Tammy at mine...dead or alive."

They picked up Jack, who gave them both a big hug, successfully transferring a stain on the front of his outfit onto both of theirs in the process. Elaine's house was in the same state of disarray they'd left it in, with breakfast dishes on the counter, toys creating an obstacle course for the houseguest, and an overflowing trashcan with a pungent odor.

"I'll start supper," said Myrtle. Surely they had eggs or something. She could handle an omelet.

"No, that's all right," said Elaine quickly. "You just have a seat. I've got it all under control." Myrtle looked suspiciously at Elaine to see if there was any hint on her face that she didn't *want* Myrtle to cook. Or didn't like her cooking. There seemed to be a misconception floating around about Myrtle's cooking. But Elaine turned her back to her and started pulling ingredients out of the fridge.

"I promise that the house isn't always a disaster," said Elaine. "Something has to give, though. It was either play with Jack yesterday or do housework. And then the funeral took up housecleaning time today, of course."

"No worries, Elaine. I'm manufacturing the mess, too." Myrtle walked to the back of the house and started a load of laundry from clothing she picked off the floor along the way. She watched the washing machine fill up. Maybe she should find some temporary help for Elaine. The cordless phone, the object of much frantic searching the day before, was conveniently located on the dryer.

"Agnes?" she asked when her friend answered. "It's Myrtle."

A stiff but polite, "Hello, there. Wasn't the service nice today?" followed a pregnant pause.

"Agnes, could you help me out? Elaine is working herself into the grave taking care of Jack, cooking, doing housework, and being proprietress at the Home for Wayward In-laws. Didn't you say you were happy with your cleaning lady? I might hire her to help Elaine for a while."

Suspicions eased, Agnes replied, "Why, that's a fine idea, Myrtle. Everybody had housekeepers when we were young mothers. I've wondered how Elaine keeps up with everything she's got going on. You don't want to lend her Puddin, I guess."

"I said I wanted to *help* Elaine. Puddin doesn't help. Getting her to even show up to clean is a job in itself. She always says her back is thrown whenever I want her to dust anything. Could your lady fit Elaine in? Who are her other clients?" Bonus points if any of the murder suspects were on her cleaning schedule. Extra bonus points if the housekeeper was chatty.

"Let's see. Jo's at Prissy's once a week, I think. She helps out Bootsie Davenport a couple of days a week, too. And she's at my house once a week."

Myrtle smiled. "She sounds *perfect*."

"I think one of her clients had to move to Greener Pastures. Maybe she can take her spot."

Agnes gave Myrtle Jo's number and hung up. Housekeepers usually were treasure troves of gossip and innuendo. Jo might know some of the same secrets Tammy knew, if she were really plugged in. Besides, Elaine could definitely use the help around the house. Myrtle hummed a bit of an old hymn. More Good Deeds.

She'd just changed out of her funeral outfit and was fixing herself something to munch on when the front door opened. Detective Lieutenant Perkins walked in with a sergeant and Red in tow. Myrtle puttered around and made a fuss over them.

To present the perfect picture of elderly innocence, she'd changed into a fluffy pink cardigan and navy pleated skirt. A large basket of knitting would have been perfect, she thought. She cursed her crafting ineptitude. But even the cardigan was pushing it as a prop, considering the triple-digit temperature. Besides, Red would have been suspicious if she poured it on *too* much. And he was already squinting distrustfully at her as it was.

Myrtle launched into a monologue of garrulous prattle. Detective Lieutenant Perkins' face remained impassive, showing not a flicker of impatience. Red, on the other hand, gaped at her, as if wondering who the woman impersonating his mother was. She was going to have to get rid of him.

Still trying to enjoy her snack, Myrtle unfortunately choked on a cracker while inhaling the air needed to fuel the chatter. As she coughed, Lieutenant Perkins took the opportunity to break in. "Mrs. Clover, I'd actually like you to tell me a little about your visit to the Beauty Box the day that Ms. Smith died." At her blank expression, he prompted patiently, "Your account of who was there and as much of the conversations and atmosphere as you can recall. It would be really helpful to me."

Red squirmed as Myrtle continued dilly-dallying, hemming, hawing and coughing. Convinced Red was about to detonate, Myrtle wondered what would push him completely over the edge. She'd rather have him kicked out of the interview than suffer his raised eyebrows, red face, and interruptions. Red was on his best behavior for Perkins' benefit and would hang out with them forever unless she could push him just a little more.

Instead of answering Perkins' question, she leaned forward, looking at him earnestly. "Agnes Walker recommended some really excellent cookies at the Piggly Wiggly. Elaine bought a bag and I'm dying to try one. Should I get us a little plate?" Sometimes a little delay was a good thing. Maybe she could redirect the conversation so that she was getting information instead of giving it. Or maybe she could push Red just a little bit...

It worked and Red finally exploded. "Mama! You've already hacked up a cracker and now you want to strangle yourself on more food? Detective Lieutenant Perkins is trying to conduct an interview here—"

Perkins cut him off, coolly. "Actually, cookies sound refreshing. Maybe you wouldn't mind getting some for us, Red." It wasn't a ques-

tion. "My sergeant could also really use your help with the suspect pro-
files."

Perkins settled back in the chair, his gray eyes steadily watching
Myrtle as her son walked to the kitchen, muttering under his breath.
Perkins' talent lay in acting as if he had all the time in the world. Instead
of hurrying to fill awkward silences, he encouraged them and the pressure that came with them.

"I don't know where to start," Myrtle said, crossly. The interview
wasn't going as planned. *She* was supposed to be interviewing *him*.

Perkins didn't offer any suggestions, so she took a deep breath and
outlined the general set-up of the beauty parlor that day—who was
there and what was said. She'd just keep any insights to herself.

Perkins nodded. "That ties in with what we've heard from the other
witnesses that day." Red brought in the plate of cookies and a pitcher
of lemonade, and then left with the sergeant while Perkins waited, still
regarding Myrtle with a thoughtful expression which was beginning to
unnerve Myrtle. She was stricken with an uncontrollable desire to come
clean. And she hadn't even done anything.

"Could you maybe provide some information about the people
who were there." He leaned forward and spoke in a voice so low that
she, too, had to lean forward to hear him. "You're a valuable resource to
me, Mrs. Clover. I need to get into these people's minds and motives to
crack this case."

Maternal pride forced her to say, "You have Red to help you out,
though. He can get into people's minds just as well as I can."

Perkins nodded. "Oh, he'll be able to give some background. But
frequently women are much more observant and insightful than men
are."

Myrtle immediately forgot her plan to keep mum. It was a relief
to talk openly about these people. A lifetime living in Bradley meant
watching your tongue, knowing that gossip would always find its way
back to the person you'd been maligning. Here was a one-time oppor-

tunity to actually vent to an eager audience who wanted every spiteful detail. She could hardly wait.

"Do I have your permission to be catty?" asked Myrtle.

"Mrs. Clover, not only do you have my permission to be catty, you have my personal request to be catty," said Perkins. He opened up a notebook.

Myrtle purred. "Well, let's see."

"Prissy Daniels?" prompted Perkins.

"Professional old-maid. She was prudish and old-fashioned by the time she was five, as I recall. Her life is wrapped up in being a preschool director and a paragon of maidenly virtue."

"Ever marry?"

"She was nobody's pretty child."

"Dina Peters?"

Myrtle sighed. "What *can* you say about Dina? She has absolutely no personality at all because she's always been stifled by people around her. Her parents were ghastly people. Bless their dead souls. Then she fell into the evil and abusive clutches of her now-ex-husband. Good-Tammy rescued her before turning into Bad-Tammy."

"How did Bad-Tammy treat Dina?"

Myrtle said, "Poorly. She either ignored her or put her down."

"Did Dina resent Tammy's behavior?"

"She doesn't seem to have the sense to resent anyone. Dina always has a vapid expression on her face. She sounded grateful if Tammy ever acknowledged her existence."

"What do you know about Kat Roberts? She's a newcomer to Bradley, right?"

Myrtle cackled. "Anyone not born in Bradley is a newcomer, if not a downright outsider. She's been in the area for a year or so but only at the Beauty Box for a couple of months. Tammy enrolled her in cosmetology school before that. As soon as she got her license, she started working with Tammy."

"Does she seem happy here? Settled?"

Myrtle said, thoughtfully, "I wouldn't call her settled. She does have a house, so she's settled into the town, but she hasn't really established her career here. She doesn't have many regulars at the Beauty Box yet. I'm sure she'd like more clientele."

Myrtle asked innocently, "Are your suspects limited to the clients at the shop? Or did Tammy manage to offend more of the general populace?"

Perkins smoothly turned the question around. "Who else do *you* think might be considered a suspect?"

Myrtle answered immediately. "Connor Walker. He had an argument with her the day she died. And Tammy's ex, Bo Smith. I'm sure ex-husbands always make a suspect list."

"They do," said Perkins. "But not in this instance. Bo Smith has an iron-clad alibi."

Then Detective Lieutenant Perkins snapped his notebook shut, leaving Myrtle with her mouth open, scrambling to turn the tables on the interview. "Thanks for your time, ma'am. Call me if you think of anything else that might be useful. Red knows how to reach me, but here's my card if you think of something else." He gave her a card with his cell phone number on it.

Before she could stammer out a protest or try a stalling tactic, he'd gone. This investigation of hers would take more legwork than she'd planned on. At least she'd learned that Tammy's ex was not on the suspect list.

Elaine walked cautiously into the den, holding Jack in one arm and a feather duster in the other. "Coast clear?"

Myrtle nodded. "All clear. Unfortunately! I didn't get a chance to get all my questions answered." Seeing Elaine reminded her about the housekeeper. What if Elaine thought she was interfering? *Was* she interfering? "Um...don't be angry with me, Elaine."

"Uh-oh. I don't like the sound of that. Are you a suspect now?"

"It's nothing to do with the case. I just thought I'd hire you a little help around the house. You know, until Jack is older and either easier to care for or can be shipped off to the Foreign Legion or something." Myrtle was horrified to see tears welling up in Elaine's eyes. "Did I hurt your feelings? The house always looks great, but when you said that you had to decide between time for you and Jack or cleaning..."

Elaine said quickly. "I'm not mad, I'm grateful. It's like having a fairy godmother." She pulled Myrtle into an enthusiastic hug, squishing a protesting Jack in the process. Then she pulled back. "It's not Puddin, is it?"

"No, no, *not* Puddin. I *like* you, Elaine. I wouldn't foist a Puddin on you. Absolutely not."

Myrtle guiltily eased out of Elaine's embrace. Well, after all, she *could* have had only the purest motives for getting the housekeeper. Did motives really matter, anyway? Wasn't it the helping that ultimately mattered in the end? She'd thought of Elaine; truly she had.

Chapter Seven

The incessant baritone baying made Myrtle turn on her bedside light. Who could sleep with the Hound of the Baskervilles roaming Bradley? No wonder Jack still needed afternoon naps. At home, used to wakeful nights, she had a pile of crossword puzzles and cryptogram books to plow through. She'd forgotten to throw her puzzle books in her suitcase. She missed her house. Stupid air conditioning company.

Surely the whole household would be up any moment. She peered at the red digital numbers on the clock radio. Two-thirty. Her stomach gurgled. But with that dog's barking, it would only be a matter of minutes that everyone would wake up. Might as well go ahead and fry up some eggs for the household.

A flabbergasted-looking Red, stumbling into the kitchen fifteen minutes later, was met by the sight of his mother wrapped in a bright red robe and flipping eggs on the stove. "Hi, Red!" she said merrily. "Come to join me? That dog must have woken you up, too."

"No, Mama. *You* woke me up when you yanked the pots and pans out. *That's* what woke me up! *You're* the only insomniac around here."

"Keep your voice down! You'll wake the whole house."

Elaine poked her head around the kitchen door. "Is everything okay?" she yawned, rubbing her eyes. Mystified, she gazed at Myrtle, now doling out eggs on plates. "What time is it? Is it time to get up?"

Red threw his hands in the air as Elaine pulled up a kitchen stool and obediently started eating the egg placed on the counter in front of her. Myrtle heard him muttering oaths as he stomped back to the bedroom.

Myrtle smiled weakly at Elaine. "Sorry—it's only two-thirty. I thought for sure that dog's howling would wake y'all up, too. Want to crawl back in bed?"

Elaine chewed a mouthful of egg. "Actually," she answered around it, "this kind of hits the spot. I wasn't sleeping well anyway. Kept thinking I heard Jack. Then I got this idea for a painting that I want to try. It just popped into my head, fully-formed. I can't wait to start working on it."

With any luck, she wouldn't be the subject of this one. Myrtle sat down and looked thoughtfully at her own plate of eggs. "Sounds wonderful, Elaine. It's nice that you've been able to explore your creativity like this. The painting looks fantastic on Miles' mantel. I let him have it over there to enjoy it while I'm staying with you."

Elaine beamed at her.

Myrtle quickly changed the subject. "Think about it, Elaine. You've been waking up tonight hearing sounds that are either real or imagined. For me, I've been kept up by a dog barking...a perfectly ordinary thing, but still enough to keep me from sleeping. So if you and I are alert to sounds that should be *expected*, what about Agnes, who lives right next door to the Beauty Box? Shouldn't she have heard a car pull up at a strange time?" She thoughtfully ate a forkful of scrambled eggs.

Elaine nodded. "Not only Agnes, but Dina. Why didn't Dina hear anything?"

"Right! She's living right in there *with* Tammy at the salon. Seems like she should have heard something when Tammy fell down the stairs. That must have made a huge racket. Tammy was a good-sized woman. See, I just don't think that we're getting the full story here. I'm going to have to ask a few questions."

"Will you?" Elaine asked.

"Of course! You know I don't like to be left in the dark on things." She took a sip of her milk and looked at Elaine over the top of the glass. "Red hasn't happened to share any information about the case with you, has he?" she asked in a quiet voice.

Elaine looked like she was trying to decide whether or not to say something. "You know it won't go any farther than me, Elaine."

"He did mention to me when we were turning in tonight that Tammy had given all her money to Dina and Kat. So it sounds like there could have been a financial motive at work, too."

"Really? I know money talks, but I wonder if Tammy really had any money," said Myrtle.

"I wondered the same thing. But Red told me that Tammy had a lot more money than he'd thought."

Enough for Dina or Kat to kill Tammy before she acted on her threat to write them out of her will?

BECAUSE MYRTLE COULDN'T really think of a good reason for a trumped-up visit with Connor Walker, she decided she'd make him a casserole. A visit would naturally go with it. While Elaine was out running errands, Myrtle spent much of the afternoon flipping through cookbooks. She skipped any recipes using time-consuming verbs like *de-bone*, *sauté*, or *mince*.

Myrtle finally found a likely candidate, but realized that she didn't have many of the ingredients. Undeterred, she substituted milk for both the cream cheese and sour cream. By five-thirty, she'd put the finishing touches on her culinary masterpiece. She carefully placed the Pyrex dish into the bottom of a sturdy tote bag. Elaine opened the back door holding Jack by the hand. "Heading out?" asked Elaine. "Looks like you've been cooking." Elaine had an anxious look on her face.

"I pulled together a chicken casserole from one of your cookbooks. I'm taking some food to poor Connor. I'm sure he's devastated by Tammy's untimely death." The hymn was a constant refrain in the back of her head.

Elaine narrowed her eyes. "He didn't seem too devastated at the funeral, as I recall."

"He's a typical man—burying his feelings. You know."

"I'm sure Mrs. Walker is taking good care of Connor. I know you're interested in poking around, but I don't want you getting hurt. And it seems to me that questioning murder suspects qualifies as dangerous."

Myrtle gave a dismissive wave. "I'm checking on him, that's all. I've known Connor since he was a tiny baby. I'm practically Auntie Myrtle. He probably feels guilty about the way things ended with Tammy and needs an elderly shoulder to cry on." Myrtle gestured to her own big-boned shoulders, which did appear designed for inconsolable sobbing.

"Just please be careful if you're nosing around. Let Red and Detective Perkins investigate. Think of Jack and how sad it would be if he had to grow up without his Nana," she said, pulling out her trump card.

Myrtle sighed. "Fine. I won't pry."

"Good idea."

As Myrtle walked towards downtown with her odd-smelling bag, Elaine noticed that two cookbook pages were stuck together by what appeared to be cream of mushroom soup. Half of *Butter Chicken Casserole* started on one page with half of *Curry Shrimp* on the next. Poor Connor.

As Myrtle walked, she glimpsed Kat, in skin-tight shorts and a tube top, rollerblading towards her from the other side of the street. Myrtle waved and Kat skated over. "Hi, Miss Myrtle," she said, with a shy smile. "Want some help with that bag?"

That virtuous feeling flashed over her again. Why not kill two birds with one stone and Do Good Deeds while investigating murder? Connor and Kat would make a remarkable couple. She'd noticed Connor staring at Kat after Tammy's funeral.

With Myrtle's mission as Cupid very clear, she did her best to appear as feeble as a tall, big-boned lady could. "Thanks, Kat. The bag was certainly starting to feel heavy."

"Where're you headed?"

"Oh, just to Connor Walker's house. Agnes' son, you know. I thought he could use a casserole. Do you know him?"

Kat shook her pink head. "No. I know he and Tammy dated, but he didn't really hang out at the Beauty Box."

"Do you think," Myrtle feebly hobbled closer to Kat, "that you could carry it for me? Just until I get to Connor Walker's house. And don't you worry, I've got a casserole coming for you soon, too! I'm hoping," said Myrtle nobly, "to offer solace to everyone who has been touched by this tragedy." She sniffed in what she considered a realistic manner.

"That's real nice of you, Miss Myrtle. My friends would have done something like that in New York, but not people I barely know. Thanks," said Kat. She looked touched, but a little embarrassed too.

Myrtle quickly said, "By the way, Kat, I love the way you did my hair last time. You're very good. And you were able to work under pressure. Tammy was really acting up."

Kat blew out a breath. "She sure was. It was making me mad, too. Drinking too much after hours is one thing, but while she was working? She should have known she was going to drive off business that way. And *my* business, too, since we're working together. What would I have done then?" An angry flush crept up Kat's neck.

"Do you know what's going to happen to the Beauty Box? Will it stay open?"

Kat gave a short laugh. "That's the funny thing. Tammy willed the shop to me. Not only that, but most of her money and other stuff. And surprisingly, she had a pretty good amount of money. Now the cops think that maybe *I* pushed Tammy down the stairs to get her money."

"But you weren't even there that night, right?"

"I bolted from the Beauty Box as fast as I could. I was sick of it and sick of Tammy. Then I was so worn out that I fell asleep right after supper," said Kat.

It wasn't much of an alibi. "I know we were all mad at Tammy that day, but it's got to have been an awful shock to have found her the next morning," said Myrtle.

They were outside Connor's house. Myrtle paused for a moment as if to rest.

Kat slowly nodded. "It was awful. I wasn't sure if Tammy had even remembered to put the dirty towels in the washer, but that was our routine. So I opened the door to the staircase...and saw her."

Kat looked directly at her. Or, actually, *down* at her, since she was taller with her rollerblades. "Your son is the police chief, isn't he? Has he mentioned anything about what they're thinking? I'm probably at the top of their suspect list."

"Red?" Myrtle gave a dry laugh. "Unfortunately, he keeps me totally out of the loop. Why do you think you're a top suspect?"

"Because of the money, mostly. I wasn't exactly swimming in money before, so maybe the cops think I bumped Tammy off to get my hands on some. Plus, there's the fact that I discovered her body. That's got to count for something, too."

Myrtle thought it *did* count for something and couldn't think of anything encouraging at all to say. She reached out and rapped sharply on Connor's door.

Luckily, Connor was home, since it hadn't occurred to her to call ahead. She'd have had to carry that casserole all the way back home, too. And it wasn't easy to use a cane and carry a casserole at the same time...even if the casserole was at the bottom of a tote bag.

Connor looked a little bemused at the appearance of both Myrtle and Kat at his door. "Ahh...hi."

Kat smiled at Connor. "Meals on wheels," she said, pointing to her rollerblades. "Miss Myrtle made a delicious casserole for you, and I'm helping her carry it."

Connor quickly stepped to the side. "Come on in. Especially if you're bringing food. And even if I'm not totally sure why you're bringing it."

Myrtle was already walking in. She'd gotten over worrying about being pushy a long time ago. Connor just wasn't one of those people she ran into a lot in Bradley, so she had to make her own opportunities. "It's a sympathy casserole," she said, carefully maneuvering around some bachelor clutter before making her way safely to a sofa. "I know your mama has explained to you that people bring food when there's a death of a loved one."

Connor still frowned. "Loved one..?"

Kat chuckled. "She means Tammy, Connor."

"And don't worry about Kat—I'm planning to put her on my casserole list, too," said Myrtle hurriedly.

"I should be heading out," said Kat, nodding at the door.

Connor smoothly interrupted, "Why not stick around for a few minutes and cool off, Kat? I've even got some Cokes in the fridge that I can pull out." Kat pulled off her skates and Connor was back in a minute with a couple of Coke cans. Myrtle was impressed enough that he had a stocked refrigerator that she was happy to overlook the lack of a glass to drink from.

"I'm delighted to get a Miss Myrtle casserole," said Connor in his deep drawl, "although I feel a little guilty accepting it. I thought that I mentioned to you at the funeral that Tammy and I weren't technically a couple anymore. In fact," he said with a sigh, "we broke up the very night she died." He looked at Kat, "Nothing against your aunt. And I do feel bad about the way things ended."

Kat shrugged. "Relationships break up every day. Besides, Tammy wasn't acting like Tammy. I'm surprised you put up with her for as long as you did."

"You did tell me about your breakup. But I'm sure that you're still hurting and feeling a lot of conflicting feelings about what happened."

"That's for sure," said Connor. "It's been pretty awful, actually."

Myrtle tried not to look too interested. "I—um—didn't realize that you'd broken up the night she died. Had you gone over to the Beauty Box, then?"

"No, we went out for dinner. I thought that Tammy wouldn't make as much of a scene if I broke up with her in public." He gave a tight smile. "I was wrong."

Kat flushed. "I bet. Tammy really turned up the volume the last couple of weeks. She was yelling over everything."

"Yelling is right...at the top of her lungs at the pizza parlor. I'm surprised you *didn't* know about the break-up, Miss Myrtle—I thought the whole town would know by now. The police sure knew about it...I'm probably their prime suspect."

Kat raised her eyebrows. "I thought *I* was their prime suspect."

"Well, I'd be delighted to be proven wrong," said Connor smoothly, with a crooked grin at Kat.

Matchmaking was going to have to wait until later—she still had some questions to ask. And this time there was no Agnes to stop her. "So when you dropped Tammy off by the Beauty Box after you broke up—that was the last time you saw her?"

"Oh, there was no dropping off, Miss Myrtle. Tammy pitched a fit and stormed out of the restaurant. I didn't drive her anywhere. But that *was* the last time I saw her. And I do feel terrible about the whole thing. We weren't right for each other, but we had some good times, too. I *liked* Tammy."

"When she was acting like Tammy," said Kat, nodding.

"Why would the police think you were a prime suspect?" asked Myrtle. "You were the one breaking up with Tammy—not the other way around."

"I had a huge fight with her that was witnessed by ten or fifteen people. They think I brooded over it, then went back to the Beauty Box and killed her. Instead, I went back home for a few beers before hitting the sack. It had been a long day."

Myrtle said, "Today's been pretty long, too. I'll leave you with the casserole, Connor." He stood up and Myrtle said, "No, don't worry about walking me out. I'm just heading back home." She ducked out quickly.

There was an awkward silence for a moment before Connor said, "It's almost dinnertime. Why don't you stay and try out some of Mrs. Clover's casserole with me. If you're not afraid to eat supper with a suspected murderer."

"I will," replied Kat, "as long as *you're* not afraid to eat supper with a fellow murder suspect."

Connor made a good host. He pulled out his good china (the plates his mother had given him), the silver (family heirlooms Agnes had entrusted to him), and a bottle of chardonnay. They reheated the casserole, put it on the plates, and toasted the meal.

Kat took the first bite, then chewed thoughtfully before spitting it out unceremoniously onto the china plate. "She's trying to kill us both! This is rank!"

Connor took a tentative bite. He stood up and deftly dumped the casserole into the garbage. "Feel like scrambled eggs and toast?" he asked.

Kat did.

Chapter Eight

Murder was good for business. The Beauty Box was packed with the curious during Myrtle's Tuesday morning wash and set. Kat allowed walk-ins for the first time in the salon's history and had to call in a couple of girls she'd met in cosmetology school to help her out.

Myrtle read a ratty copy of *Good Housekeeping* while waiting her turn. Dina Peters touched up Agnes' manicure and wistfully mentioned wanting to start styling and dyeing hair. Bootsie Davenport chatted loudly on her cell phone while Prissy fumbled in her patent-leather pocketbook for what appeared to be a pitiful tip.

Tammy's murder was definitely the two-thousand-pound gorilla in the room. Ordinarily, these women would be full of gossip about Tammy's death. Their polite silence must be because no one wanted to upset Kat. Or maybe Dina, since she already appeared on the verge of tears.

It would probably be healthier, thought Myrtle virtuously, if they didn't tiptoe around the subject. Prissy was conveniently close and was still trying to pull her things together. Myrtle said, "Prissy, could you visit with me for a few minutes?"

Prissy blinked in confusion. Myrtle said, "I guess I'm just being fanciful, but the Beauty Box has a different aura today—sort of spooky. It makes me feel dithery. Some conversation might help distract me a little."

Agnes' eyes narrowed suspiciously, not knowing anyone less inclined to dithering than Myrtle. Prissy gazed longingly at the door before obediently sitting next to Myrtle.

"It's awful, isn't it? It makes a body wonder what this world is coming to." Prissy's shiver seemed more excited than frightened.

Myrtle scanned the Beauty Box to see if any guilty faces peered her way. She hoped to have one anguished soul yearning to unload its ghastly secrets. To her disappointment, the roaring air conditioner and the droning domed dryers drowned out her conversation with Prissy.

Myrtle cupped her ear. "I've forgotten to put in my hearing aid this morning. Can't hear a thing without my ears. Could you speak up for me, sweetie?" she yelled.

Prissy cleared her throat. "I *said* that I wonder what this world is *coming* to." She clicked her false teeth nervously.

Myrtle bellowed, "That poor girl. Killed right in the prime of her life."

Regulars and walk-ins stared at Myrtle with interest. She looked innocently around the room, gauging reactions to the high-volume conversation. Kat said mildly, "Tammy wasn't exactly what I'd call a helpless victim, Miss Myrtle."

Could this conversation even be heard above the din? Myrtle shrugged helplessly. "Could someone translate, loudly? I forgot my ears this morning."

Bootsie Davenport rolled her eyes. "Tammy was sweet and sour, Myrtle. And we saw nothing but sour lately. Nobody's crying themselves to sleep over Tammy."

Dina Peters burst into noisy sobbing. "But she was my only friend and I miss her. Oh, Tammy!" She flung her head down on the manicure table, frizzy curls quivering with histrionics.

Agnes Walker patted Dina gingerly, trying not to smear newly-applied Cocktail Carnival red polish on Dina's thin shoulder. "Dina, everything will work out—you'll see. Here, you mentioned wanting to experiment with dyeing. Want me to schedule an appointment with you? The only way to move ahead in this world is to try new things."

This was very rash of Agnes and just went to show how desperate she was to distract Dina. Hopefully she was planning on Dina coloring her hair gray or slightly blue. She couldn't imagine the old lady as a blonde or redhead. Dina blinked at her, thinking it over, then started howling again before running out of the room.

Agnes frowned reprovingly at Myrtle. "Look what you've done now! You're meddling, Myrtle. Did you have to bring up the topic of Tammy?"

"I'm not meddling. I'm simply talking about what happened."

Agnes glowered at Myrtle. "I think you need a vacation, Myrtle Clover."

Myrtle smiled brightly. "Want to come with me?"

"No, I do not, as you well know. I told you my traveling days are over." Agnes whipped a book from her pocketbook, reading it with determination.

The customers were silent for a few minutes before the idle chatter resolutely resumed. This was the South, where outbursts were politely ignored first and gossiped over later. Prissy, all genteel confusion, had exited. Bootsie admired her fresher, less matronly, Kat-inspired hairdo until her cell phone belted out its rap song ringtone. Agnes blew on her nails to dry them. Myrtle regarded the visit as a total bust. The exception came when Kat received a bouquet of flowers and a card that made her blush. At least her matchmaking was working out well. She hummed the old hymn under her breath.

Myrtle picked up *Good Housekeeping* again, flipping to the recipes. Finding a tasty prospect, she scanned the shop furtively, tore the page out, and stuck it in her bottomless pocketbook. You just never knew when another in-sympathy casserole might be necessary.

MYRTLE OFFERED TO LISTEN out for Jack, who was napping, while Elaine ran errands. It was also time for *Tomorrow's Promise*, which was Myrtle's favorite soap opera. Red came through the back door, looking grouchy and hungry. He opened his mouth to say something to Myrtle, but she lifted her hand to hush him. Soleil was just about to tell Rohan that she'd always loved him...and she wasn't about to miss it.

When the commercial break started, Myrtle joined Red in the kitchen. "This is a late lunch, isn't it?"

Red grunted. "And I didn't get breakfast. I can't wait until this case wraps up."

"Early start this morning?"

Red glowered at her. "No earlier than you, Mama. Did you ever go back to bed after your two-thirty jaunt in the kitchen?"

"No, I was wide awake. Who knows—I might join Jack for a nap later." She paused for a moment. "Gotten any closer to identifying the killer?"

Red answered cautiously, "We've got a few ideas."

"The M.O. makes it look like the perp is a novice, doesn't it?"

"Why, yes, Mama. The murderer's a real greenhorn. Did you think there's a Mafia hit man terrorizing Bradley?" His eyes were hard slits. "Perp? M.O.? You watching *Murder, She Wrote* reruns on cable again?"

"What if I am?" Myrtle gave him a disdainful look. Red had never given Jessica Fletcher her proper due.

Red held up his hand. "I don't have time to argue, Mama. Got to grab a quick lunch before heading back to work."

Myrtle gave a look that she hoped was just polite interest.

Red looked at Myrtle sideways like he was trying to figure out whether he should tell her something. "Detective Lieutenant Perkins wants to go back and question some folks again and wants me to join him. Says I should know how to approach the suspects and what they might be trying to hide." Red sighed. "I don't have a clue what was going on in these people's private lives, Mama. I think this town is chock-full of secrets, too."

It would be better if this ended up being *Red's* idea. Red pulled mayo, mustard, lettuce and roast beef out of the fridge. Slathering bread with Hellmann's, he said, "Hey, Mama, hear any juicy gossip while you were hanging out at the Beauty Box? Did you know who Tammy was picking on or what dirt she was holding over their heads?"

"Well, I *did* hear some gossip," said Myrtle, in a tantalizing way. "Was there anybody in *particular* you were looking for information about?"

"Okay, let me tell you who we're looking at...but don't spread private police business all over town. We've talked to Prissy Daniels a couple of times, which you probably already know since every busybody in town was dangling out their windows when our car pulled in front of Miss Prissy's house. We'll drop in on Bootsie Davenport next. Both ladies have been evasive."

Red took a bite from his sandwich and mumbled through it, "We got nowhere with Prissy. She kept spilling her tea all over the table, which made me wonder why she was so nervous. What do you know about her? I just know she taught me Sunday school when I was a teenager."

"Prissy was probably just nervous because you were at her house. No man has probably ever passed through her door. Tammy *was* being snide about her, though."

Red leaned forward on the kitchen stool. "Do you remember exactly what Tammy said?"

"Tammy was just taunting everybody—sort of a cat and mouse thing. She was making fun of Prissy as soon as she walked out the door. Prissy, as usual, forgot something and came back in the shop to overhear Tammy snickering over 'our Prissy. She's not as sweet as she looks.'"

"What dirt could anybody possibly find on Prissy Daniels?"

"Maybe she's a closet alcoholic with a DUI in her past? Maybe it's something scandalous that would really mess up her gig at Little Lambs Preschool. That preschool is her favorite place in the world. She's always asking people at the Beauty Box if they want to come by and tell stories to the kids there."

"A DUI? I've never even seen Prissy Daniels drink root beer. And the DUI, if there was one, didn't happen in my jurisdiction." Red rubbed the palms of his hands over his eyes. "It's the end of the world if Miss Prissy is an alkie. What next? Bootsie Davenport was abducted by aliens?"

"According to Tammy, something a lot more human abducted Bootsie. She supposedly has some young man she's seeing. Someone mentioned to me that she thought it was Connor."

Red grunted noncommittally, but raised his eyebrows.

"Agnes' son is the only lothario I can think of," added Myrtle, studying Red. He looked like he might know something about Bootsie's love life.

"Connor must've had his hands full with Tammy."

"Tammy was enough to keep anybody busy," Myrtle agreed. "I don't know if Connor was cheating on Tammy or not. I don't know whom Bootsie is seeing, but Tammy seemed pretty sure it was *someone*."

"I really don't see Connor being interested in Bootsie," said Red.

Myrtle felt a touch of guilt over Kat. Had she sent a pink-haired lamb to the slaughter? What if Connor were some kind of lady-killer...for real? "I guess you're right. He's probably just not ready to settle down.

This conversation with Red wasn't going as well as it should. He was giving her some hints as to whom they were interested in investigating closer, but she was talking too much. What she needed was some fresh information. And another cop. "Red, I was thinking, why don't you invite Detective Lieutenant Perkins over to supper tonight? He's a visitor to Bradley, after all, and it would be the polite thing to do."

Red peered at her through squinty eyes. "You're not planning to pump him for information, are you?"

She looked down her nose at him. "Of course not. We should extend our hospitality, that's all." Thunder rumbled ominously outdoors, and Red frowned at her suspiciously.

"Well, I don't know. It's kind of last minute for Elaine."

Myrtle said, "I'll call Elaine's cell phone real quick—she was going to finish up her errands at the store. She could pick up some food from the grocery store deli: fried chicken, coleslaw, potato salad, fruit. I'll even pay for it!" She felt very benevolent. "Oh, and Miles can come, too. You know how he enjoys going out for dinner."

Red sighed. "I guess so. Thanks for hijacking my quiet evening."

Myrtle acted as demure as a very big-boned woman could. "You know, Red, I've been meaning to drop by and visit with Prissy for a while. Just to see about volunteering to read for the preschool classes," she hurried on as Red opened his mouth to object. "After all," she said with a sanctimonious air, "it's important to give something back to the community."

Red politely overlooked that his mother had been immune to the need for community involvement for the past eighty years. "You're messing with a hornets' nest."

"I'm visiting *Prissy*, that's all. She's hardly a homicidal maniac. Besides, she'll actually *talk* to me. When you were there, she was probably too stunned to even say anything."

"Be careful, Mama."

It was the second warning she'd received that day. But humming the hymn put the warning right out of her head.

Prissy's cottage was just a short walk from Red and Elaine's house. Myrtle strolled down the sidewalk through downtown Bradley. The old street was divided by a grassy median with a row of dogwoods down the center. The streetlights flanking the road were hung with American flags. What could have been hokey in another town was perfect for

Bradley. She gave an appreciative sniff as she passed Bo's Diner, packed with the lunchtime crowd. She walked by the small city hall with the fountain in front and took a left down the next street.

Prissy's little yard was plucked, pruned and manicured with luscious zoysia grass, yellow Jessamine enthusiastically climbing her fence and English ivy scaling the shady side of the house. Steep concrete stairs climbed to the cheery red front door. Myrtle took a deep breath and carefully mounted the steps. They were even steeper than they'd looked, and she gasped for breath as she leaned against Prissy's buzzer.

Prissy answered the door, bleating in distress as Myrtle wobbled on the porch. "Myrtle! You shouldn't climb those stairs. If you'd called ahead, I'd have met you in the yard..." and so on while pulling her inside with hands much stronger than they appeared. To Myrtle's dismay, Prissy was yelling at full volume. Myrtle remembered that she'd claimed deafness in the beauty parlor. "Got my ears in now, Prissy!"

Prissy ushered her into a prim parlor where Prissy's dead ancestors glared reprovingly from the walls. The scent of lemon oil polish competed with a faint smell of mothballs hanging in the air. A well-worn Queen Anne chair and an old-fashioned settee gave a half-hearted welcome. Myrtle gratefully plopped on the settee, accompanied by a screech of springs. Prissy, still fussing, perched her cadaverous figure on the edge of a chair.

This didn't need to be a *long* visit. She'd just launch into her spiel. "I wanted to see if you needed a storyteller at the Little Lambs Preschool. I know you've mentioned it a few times at the beauty parlor. I could volunteer once every week or two and read to the children," said Myrtle.

Prissy's face brightened at her offer. Now Myrtle felt guilty. She'd go to the church and read to the little urchins, after all. Maybe she could check out the program while she was there and see if it might work for Jack.

While Prissy extolled the virtues of storytelling, the preciousness of the preschool and of children in general, Myrtle stole glances around the room. It was painstakingly neat with a Spartan lack of clutter. Myrtle was disappointed the parlor's tables weren't littered with love letters, poison pen mail or smoking guns. Myrtle gazed longingly through a door that appeared to lead to Prissy's bedroom and bathroom.

Myrtle interrupted Prissy's reverent monologue. "Prissy, I hope you don't mind, but I need to use your powder room."

Prissy said, "Of course, Myrtle! The bathroom connects to my bedroom."

Myrtle walked through a narrow hall to a small bedroom. At first, Myrtle saw nothing interesting about the room. The bed was covered in an attractive old spread that looked like an heirloom. A handmade quilt from the same era was folded neatly at the foot of the bed. There were two clutter-free bedside tables. Myrtle was about to give up in disgust at the anonymous neatness of the room when she spotted a desk in the corner of the room with a computer on top.

She was halfway across the room when she heard the squeaking of floorboards in the hall and hurried to the bathroom instead. She shut the door quickly behind her and flushed the john. Then she washed her hands in the porcelain washstand, drying them on dainty finger towels hanging next to the sink. Was Prissy hovering out in the hall, making sure Myrtle wasn't snooping?

Myrtle made sure the coast was clear before hurrying back into the bedroom. Prissy called after her, "Miss Myrtle? Everything all right?"

She's checking up on me. "Just fine, Prissy. As I *told you*, I needed to use your powder room all of a sudden. No reason for alarm."

There wasn't enough time. She'd have to find a reason for a follow-up visit. And a reason for a second bathroom visit. *Plus* a way to distract Prissy for a longer time. As she walked back into the living room, Prissy gave her a weak smile. Myrtle felt reassured. Prissy had no reason to suspect her, after all. She was in the bedroom legitimately and hadn't touched the computer.

"Prissy, I'm so impressed! I'd no idea you were computer savvy. Red and Elaine have one of those contraptions, but they're young people. I just don't have a clue on those machines."

She'd expected Prissy to preen at the praise and register that supposedly computer illiterate Myrtle wouldn't be hacking into the thing, but instead Prissy turned a mottled red color. She must really have some dirty stuff on there. Myrtle threw Prissy a lifeline. "You use it for school email and that type of thing?"

Prissy spluttered out gibberish. Since she obviously wasn't going to regain her composure anytime soon, Myrtle promised to check into reading to the preschool children and, carefully balancing on her cane, slowly descended the steep stairs. She felt Prissy's eyes burning into her back as she left.

Chapter Nine

Detective Lieutenant Perkins was no fool— a fact that was very irritating indeed. Myrtle very delicately brought up a couple of questions, and he'd said, "No offense, Mrs. Clover, but I'd rather enjoy this delicious supper and forget about work tonight." Myrtle finally gave up in disgust and concentrated on the fried chicken and the crumbly corn bread muffins.

Elaine and Red gamely made conversation with the stern-faced Perkins. After a few minutes, he loosened up and quick intelligence and dry humor surfaced. Too bad he took his work so seriously.

After supper and dessert, Myrtle excused herself and went into the den to play with Jack. Red nodded his head towards his mother and said to Detective Lieutenant Perkins out of the corner of his mouth, "Don't let Mama fool you. She's smart as they come. Buys those New York Times crossword puzzle books by the dozens and knocks them out in minutes. Took the Mensa tests for fun and blew the top right off of them."

"Really?" Perkins was impressed but not surprised. Red was sharp, too, and Perkins figured his good-old-boy act was just a front.

Myrtle returned to the dining room, saying crossly, "Red, where's the remote? Elaine says she taped *Tomorrow's Promise* this afternoon and I can't find the thing anywhere."

Perkins smiled at Red's sheepish expression. "She can't always watch *Masterpiece Theater*," Red mumbled.

THE ONLY POSITIVE PART of the night was that the combination of fattening Southern food and boring conversation had given Myrtle her first good night's sleep in a long while. The next morning Red greeted her at the breakfast table with a smile. "Just got a call on my cell from the air conditioning people, Mama. They're going to be at your house in twenty minutes. I'm going over there to let them in and talk with them about the system."

He looked pleased as punch. It made Myrtle feel a little sour. She hadn't even gotten the information she wanted on the case, yet. It was all very discouraging.

After she'd eaten and gotten dressed, she looked out the window and saw Red talking with the repairmen.

There was a rap at Elaine's front door. She pulled it open and saw dumpy Puddin standing on her front step with a baleful look on her pale face. "Puddin! What are you doing here!"

"Went over to your house, didn't I? To clean? And Red sent me over here to talk to you."

"You're not even supposed to clean my house for another few days. Are you sick or something?" It was a record show of productivity for the lazy Puddin. Myrtle would have to make it a red letter day in her diary.

"Just thought I'd clean." Puddin ambled in and plopped down on Elaine's sofa, ready to visit.

"Puddin, I don't have time for your foolishness today. You have the worst timing of anyone I've ever seen. I haven't even been over at my house to make a mess. The air conditioner is broken."

"Beauty Box doesn't need me right now and this was one of my days over there. Kat doesn't need a cleaner, she says." She rolled her eyes.

"Probably because Kat works harder than Tammy did. I'm sure she's doing her own cleaning now." Or maybe she was tired of Puddin's nonsense. "Well, today isn't a good day to clean at my house. Come back again on your normal day."

Puddin gave her a resentful look. "All right, I'm going. Maybe Mr. Connor's house needs a cleaning."

Myrtle raised her eyebrows. "I didn't know you were cleaning for Connor Walker. When did this happen?" If Puddin were Connor's housekeeper, that would explain why his house was so messy.

Puddin relaxed into the sofa a little more. "Since his house started being dirty."

"He's a bachelor. His house must have been dirty for years."

"He just started caring about it a few months ago. And I saw something interesting there yesterday." Puddin's grin showed a broken tooth. "He had *company* there!"

"What kind of company?"

"*Kat* was there!" said Puddin in triumph.

"Overnight?"

"Naw," said Puddin, waving her hand in dismissive fashion. "But during the day."

This wasn't the news Myrtle was hoping to be able to get from Puddin. Particularly since she'd already known this news. And, actually, since she was instrumental in causing this news to even exist."

Puddin must have realized that her gossip wasn't impressing Myrtle. "Something else I know," she added quickly. "Heard it from another cleaner who I know. She knows someone who knows someone..."

"Puddin!" said Myrtle in a threatening tone.

"...who cleans for Miz Bootsie," finished Puddin triumphantly as if proud of her close connections. "She says that Miz Bootsie has secrets."

This was not good enough information to justify an intrusive visit from Puddin. "I've got secrets, myself. Plenty of stuff that I don't want anybody to know. Like what's in my medicine cabinets, how much I weigh, what my shoe size is, since my feet aren't exactly dainty—"

Puddin was shaking her head scornfully. "This is a better secret. Miz Bootsie has a boyfriend. That's what they say," she said defensively, as if she couldn't quite believe it herself.

Interesting. Maybe Tammy had been on to something, after all. She'd have to see what she could get out of Bootsie's cleaner, when it was time for her to visit Elaine's house.

By the time Myrtle had finally shooed Puddin out of the house, it was nearly lunchtime. Looking out the window, it appeared that the repairmen were still milling around and that the air conditioner hadn't been fixed. Myrtle was feeling like some fried food and Bo's Diner was just the place. It helped that the diner was owned by Tammy's ex and was a mecca for local gossip and news.

A bell rang as she opened the door to the diner. Myrtle breathed in the smell of fried vegetables appreciatively. The décor at the diner hadn't changed since Bo took it over from his father twenty years ago. Its dark wood-paneled walls, green Formica-topped tables and lunch counter, and the scrubbed-clean linoleum floors had an un-touristy feel that pleased the locals. An old Coke promotional sign proclaimed "Breakfast served anytime" and "If you can't say it to Granny, please don't say it in here."

Myrtle glanced around the small restaurant and saw Bootsie sitting with Judge Davenport at a table in the back. They fell into the category of old married couples with nothing to say to each other. They'd talked every possible conversation and weren't creative enough people to develop new lines of discussion.

Conveniently, there were no empty tables. With a wobbly gait, Myrtle approached the Davenports' booth. She asked in a feeble voice, "Could I share a table with y'all? I'd try the lunch counter stools, but. . ." Myrtle shrugged helplessly.

Judge Beauregard Davenport rose hastily to his feet and Bootsie urged, "Sit with us, sweetie."

Myrtle winced at the familiarity. She preferred old-school deferential treatment with lots of ma'ams thrown in for good measure. She gritted her teeth and managed a grimaced smile in return as she slid onto the vinyl booth next to Bootsie.

Beauregard said, "Glad you could sit with us, Miss Myrtle. We wouldn't want you hoistin' yourself up at the lunch counter stool. How're you doing? Bootsie, did you know Miss Myrtle taught me eleventh grade English?"

Bootsie seemed stunned that her elderly husband had ever been in eleventh grade. Myrtle said, "I wasn't much older than my students that year. One of my very first years on the job." Small talk followed along the themes of Beauregard's youthful indiscretions, and Bootsie appeared relieved at her escape from a silent lunch.

Myrtle's order was quickly taken and served, despite the crowd. When asked her view on Greener Pastures, Myrtle happily offered her opinion on retirement homes in general ("It's fun living with your peers in college, but depressing when your peers are geriatric—") before detailing the specific iniquities committed by Greener Pastures' cafeteria staff. Myrtle assured them the meatloaf, fried okra, black-eyed peas, and bread pudding at Bo's Diner were *far* superior to food at Greener Pastures. Gesturing emphatically with her fork, Myrtle shared her theory that the food woes at Greener Pastures were symptomatic of larger problems at the facility.

Bootsie frowned, revealing tiny little wrinkles. "Mama never mentioned the food being that bad. Should we have lunch with her Sunday after church?" she asked her husband.

"I wouldn't go Sunday," said Myrtle with a knowledgeable air. "They serve the finest food of the week then because that's the day everyone visits." She leaned forward confidentially. "They'll have chicken. They should call it rubber chicken because they'll stretch that sucker all the way through the week. Chicken salad. Chicken tacos. Fried chicken. Chicken surprise." Myrtle shook her head. "Go Friday night. That'll be an eye-opener."

Judge Davenport pulled at his shirt collar a little bit. He probably didn't fancy removing his mother-in-law from the reasonably priced Greener Pastures and depositing her in The Belk Home for the Aged, at much steeper costs. Myrtle had a feeling he'd be changing the subject very quickly. He looked like he was wracking his brain for better conversation topics.

"Hear anything from Red about how Tammy Smith's case is going?" he asked.

Bootsie rolled her eyes. "Tammy again! I'm tired of that subject, darling," she implored him. "Her death was actually the best thing that could have happened to the Beauty Box. With Kat in charge, it'll be so much cuter. And have *real* beauticians." She said the last sentence pointedly as Dina wandered into the diner with fuzzy pink curlers in her hair before realizing her mistake with horror as people stared at her and darting out the door again.

"I only want to know how Red's getting on," he protested.

Myrtle interrupted the argument, not wanting to let the chance pass, "I think the investigation is going pretty well. He said they had some new leads. He wouldn't tell me what they were, though."

Judge Davenport scraped up the last bit of macaroni and cheese off his plate. "Did they find anyone with a grudge against Tammy Smith?"

Something resembling a snort came from his ladylike wife. Myrtle answered, "Everybody she came in regular contact with had a grudge against her." Myrtle dipped her head closer to her Blue Plate special and surreptitiously watched Bootsie through her eyelashes. "Tammy knew a lot of secrets and her drinking made her a loudmouth." With an innocent look, she sat back up and asked, "Don't you agree, Bootsie?"

Bootsie turned pale, then flushed. "I suppose, Miss Myrtle," she replied slowly. She squinted shrewdly at Myrtle. Bootsie wouldn't want to give up the easy life she had with her husband. Could she kill someone though? She probably could, given the right circumstances. If she felt like her back was against the wall.

"And poor Connor Walker and his broken heart," said Myrtle, shaking her head sorrowfully.

She didn't really get the reaction she was hoping for. Bootsie and her husband merely looked surprised at the change of subject. Bootsie answered, "Were they all that close, Miss Myrtle? I had the impression that things were cooling off between them."

Maybe Connor wasn't the young man in Bootsie's life, after all. Bootsie resumed her bored moue until her cell phone loudly announced its presence, and she eagerly grabbed it from her designer purse. Judge Davenport finished his lunch, and said with automatic endearment to his wife, when she'd wrapped up her conversation, "Sweetheart, are you ready to head out? Miss Myrtle, it was a pleasure."

Bootsie rose and picked up her pocketbook. "Yes, it was. And thanks for giving me the heads-up on the Home, honey. We'll be sure to go over and check on Mama."

Myrtle smiled as the suddenly glum Beauregard Davenport followed his wife from the diner. His wallet would soon be a lot lighter. Myrtle doubted Bootsie would be impressed by the Friday night supper offerings at Greener Pastures.

The diner was at its lunchtime busiest, and Bo Smith, the owner of the diner, came out of the kitchen to help check on tables. When he reached Myrtle's, he leaned his large frame over and spoke deferentially. "Everything okay, Miss Myrtle?"

She studied his open face and wondered again why Tammy had been so mean to him. He wasn't handsome like Connor, but tall and bulky with a belly sneaking over his beltline. His nose wasn't perfectly straight and his hairline had receded into a memory. But he was hardworking, loyal, and sweet. Much as Tammy had wanted to play victim, Myrtle was certain Bo wouldn't have laid a finger on her.

"Everything's delicious as usual, Bo. But I should be asking *you* if everything's okay. Tammy's death must have come as a shock to you."

To Myrtle's discomfort, Bo's eyes welled with tears. "Aw, Miss Myrtle," he said, rubbing a beefy scrubbed-raw hand over his face. "Things are awful, just awful." Despite the bustle around him, he was eager to talk and pulled out a chair to sit with her. "She was so full of life! It don't seem right she's dead." He sniffed loudly.

"My friends tell me Tammy wouldn't have shed any tears over me. I know she told stories about me around town." He gave Myrtle an imploring look. "I never laid a finger on her. I cherished every hair on her little head. She just didn't want anybody to think she was a loser, even at marriage. She liked being the strong one. I know that was the reason she said all those things. I let her tell people I was the bad guy if it helped her save face." He stared blankly out the window. "Then she started going with Mrs. Walker's son, Connor."

"That must have been hard on you."

"It sure was. But not as hard as the news that Tammy died."

Myrtle tiptoed delicately around the alibi. "You didn't happen to see or hear anything the night of her murder? The diner isn't too far away from the salon."

"No, I sure didn't. That was our late night for being open and we were short staffed. It was past midnight by the time I left here, and the police told me that Tammy was already gone then." He fished around in his pocket for a tissue.

That was the solid alibi that Perkins had alluded to. And she'd learned more about the time of death, too. "I didn't even realize that y'all were open that late. Whatever you're doing with the diner has really made it successful, though. It's always packed in here."

Bo gazed with blind eyes around the restaurant. "The reason I worked so hard after the divorce is because I was trying to forget about Tammy. Slaving days was the only way I could sleep nights."

"'*I worked like a horse and I ate like a hog and I slept like a dead man*,'" quoted Myrtle understandingly.

Bo's kind face creased with wrinkles of concern. He studied Myrtle as if worried he was witnessing the first signs of dementia. She reassured, "Kipling."

The name didn't seem to register with him. Myrtle moved on, "Do you think that Connor could have murdered Tammy? I hear they had quite an argument the night she died."

Bo shook his head. "But it wouldn't have been easy to get rid of Tammy. She'd have been furious at being dumped. Maybe she'd have fought about it, especially if she'd been drinking. He could've pushed her a little to shut her up." He sighed. "She was a lot smaller than you'd have thought. No bigger than a minute. Maybe he just shoved her and she fell down those stairs."

Myrtle felt it was kinder not to mention the scissors embedded in Tammy's back. And Tammy *wasn't* little. Maybe she was just little compared to Bo.

One of Bo's waitresses punched him on the shoulder as she went by. "Bo! We need some help with this crowd. The orders in the kitchen are getting backed up, too."

Bo sighed and stood up. "Gotta run, Miss Myrtle. But it was nice talking to you, ma'am." He gave a shy smile.

"Nice talking to you, too, Bo. Tell your mother hi for me. I haven't seen her in ages."

She was about to go pay at the front desk when she saw Kat walk through the door and look around for a table. Since there were still none available, Myrtle gestured for her to sit next to her. Kat grinned, her pink hair glinting in the sun beaming through the window. "Perfect timing, huh?"

Myrtle noticed from the corner of her eye that Connor Walker walked in through the diner door. Once again she motioned to share the table. As he sauntered over, she said to Kat, "Yes, dear, I think it is." As soon as Connor reached the table and pulled out a chair, Myrtle glanced at her watch and dithered, "Is that *really* the time? I've got to run. Delicious lunch! I do recommend the Blue Plate special today." Connor stood back up respectfully, handed Myrtle her cane, and watched as she paid at the front counter. The hymn replayed in her head again. Saint Myrtle. It had a nice ring to it.

Connor sat back down and looked across the table at a sardonically smiling Kat. "Maybe she's trying to make up for nearly killing us with that casserole," said Kat.

Connor answered sheepishly, "I guess she's matchmaking. She's as bad as my mother." He would have to pay Miss Myrtle back for all her helpfulness. "What'll we order?"

Chapter Ten

Myrtle, stiff from sitting so long in the diner, walked slowly back to Red's house. Old age's peculiarities, infirmities, and indignities never ceased to amaze her. She was relieved when Elaine pulled up next to her in the minivan. "Going my way?" she called to Myrtle out the window.

"Sweetie, I'll go anywhere *you're* going, if I can ride there."

"Jump in. I'm headed back home, but your ride might not be as restful as you thought." As Myrtle gingerly climbed into the van, she heard a high-pitched yell emitting from her grandson's mouth. Elaine rolled her eyes. "He needs a nap."

"Do you have more errands to run? I'm going to put my feet up for a little while. If you take us home, I'll put him down and watch my soaps while you shop. Might as well take advantage of my being here. It looks like my air is going to be fixed later today."

"Thanks, Myrtle. Errands take twice as long with getting Jack in and out of the car seat. Jack never wants to get *in* the car seat, then he never wants to be taken out again! If you're watching *Tomorrow's Promise,* hit 'record' for me, would you? I'll catch it later." Elaine drove them back to the house and they all walked inside. Elaine pulled a bunch of coupons out of a kitchen drawer, grabbed the grocery circular, and hurried out the door.

Myrtle glanced at the clock. She eased onto the sofa, shook off her shoes, and put her feet on the coffee table. She found the record button on the remote and pushed it.

Soaps were a guilty pleasure. The writing was frequently horrid, the acting worse. But there was just something about them that drew her in. Babies born mere episodes ago might now be precocious toddlers to fit the needs of the scriptwriters.

She clucked at the television. Sally, married to the obnoxious bully Stone, finally left him, embarking on a similarly dependent relationship with obsessively jealous Wesley. Myrtle shook her head. The show's writers obviously thought their audience gullible enough to believe these plots.

The doorbell rang. Myrtle scowled at the buzz, hoping it hadn't awakened Jack. An angry roar indicated it had. Myrtle cursed at her cane, propped unhelpfully across the room, and tried pulling up with the aid of the coffee table. Her efforts took a long time and the doorbell rang again. Gritting her teeth, she finally stood up, wobbling to the front door and opening it in time to prevent Dina Peters from pushing the doorbell for a third time.

Dina stared miserably at the breathless Myrtle. She absently pushed her large, pink glasses to the top of her small nose. "Miss Myrtle, I'm so sorry. I wondered if the doorbell worked at all. You know how sometimes you just ring and ring a bell and no one comes? I wondered, "Should I ring the bell again? Should I knock? Is knocking worse than ringing?"

Dina's tremulous voice warbled on while Myrtle panted and motioned her in. When she'd finally gotten her breath back she beamed at Dina as if she were delighted to see her. "Dina, dear! No worries. You're not putting me out one bit. I'm not sure *why* I sat on Red's ridiculous sofa when I know I have trouble getting off of it. I *must* remember to keep that cane nearby. Now, let's see. Coca-Colas for both of us, right?

And ginger snaps from the pantry." Myrtle grimaced as Jack grew more insistent.

Dina offered, "I'll follow the hollering and get him, Miss Myrtle." She disappeared to the back of the house, but by the time Myrtle was returning with snacks and drinks, she was quickly returning with a suspicious Jack, who held Dina's finger with one hand and clutched Dirty Doggy with the other. Jack let go of both when he saw the food, grabbing the cookies and disappearing back to his room to eat his treasure.

"I haven't seen *Tomorrow's Promise* for so long," Dina breathed, settling down on the sofa next to Myrtle. "Did Tristan and Pamela get married yet?"

Myrtle sniffed. "*Married*? Sweetheart, they were married, had four kids and divorced."

Dina was shocked. "In three weeks?"

"You know how fast things go on soaps."

"Did Timothy break away from that satanic cult?"

Myrtle caught her up on the twisted lives of the major characters. Stone pounded on Sally's door, demanding that she return to his abuse and dump the equally abusive Wesley.

At the commercial, Myrtle turned her attention back to Dina and blinked to see her face flushed with fury. "He can't treat Sally that way," she fumed. "Too bad Sally doesn't have a friend like Tammy. Tammy saved me from my ex and really supported me. She'd been abused by Bo."

"Tammy wasn't abused, Dina. Bo's a good and decent man."

"No, Miss Myrtle. He's wicked." She sniffed. "Actually, that's the reason why I'm here. I'm giving the money Tammy left me to the battered women's shelter. I'm visiting my neighbors to raise money. I was planning on asking Elaine for donations, but I'll hit you up since you're here."

Dina spoke with a passionate zeal that Myrtle had formerly only heard when she defended Tammy.

"You must be so pleased, dear, to have a bequest from Tammy. I know she mentioned it that day in the Beauty Box—of course, though, that was one of Tammy's bad days."

There was an angry flash in Dina's eyes that she quickly hid. "I knew Tammy had set something aside for me, but I had no idea it was as much as it was." Dina's jaw set stubbornly. "She was a very generous person, you know."

Myrtle nodded. "Well, and you are too, helping out the shelter. Let me pull out my pocketbook and write you a check." Jack had wandered back in and was captivated by a fiery argument on the screen. Myrtle fumbled with the remote until Sesame Street came obligingly on.

Dina gave her an earnest smile. "Thanks for the check, Miss Myrtle. Donated items for the shelter would be great, too, if you or Elaine could pick up some extra tubes of toothpaste while you're at the store or give us your old paperback books, clothes—things like that." Myrtle promised to round up some contributions from the considerable clutter at her home and drop them off at the Beauty Box for Dina to take to the shelter.

Dina kept talking happily while Myrtle made out her check. Dina wasn't so bad. Oh, she was a little annoying with her preachy voice, and she certainly didn't make the most of her appearance. But at least she'd finally hit on something that gave her a feeling of self-worth. And she hadn't had to go through a man or a bullying friend to get it.

Actually, Dina might make a decent match for Bo, come to think of it. It was time to Do More Good. "Have you tried the diner yet, Dina?" Seeing Dina's confusion, Myrtle added, "I bet if you asked Bo nicely, he'd let you put a big jar on the counter with a sign asking for spare change for the shelter."

Dina looked horrified. "I couldn't have anything to do with that man. Tammy told terrible stories about him." She absently picked up Jack's Dirty Doggy and gave it a squeeze, as if to get a little reassurance from the stuffed doll. Jack quietly said, "Mine," under his breath, as if practicing for the moment when he'd have to get his friend back from the crazy visitor.

Stories was right. "Bo isn't as bad as you thought and the diner is the most popular place in town. You'd raise a bundle for the new shelter."

Reluctantly, Dina agreed. "Well, I don't know. I guess I could. For the sake of the shelter, of course." Dina thanked Myrtle and headed out the door. Jack yelled, "Mine!" and Myrtle realized that Dina had absconded with Dirty Doggy. After rescuing the stuffed animal from its kidnapper, Myrtle sat back down—in the armchair this time—and caught the rest of *Tomorrow's Promise* while Jack miraculously snoozed on the quilt, a death-grip on Dirty Doggy.

Myrtle must have dozed off, too, because she jumped violently at the shrill ring of the phone. Cursing and hoping that Jack was a sound sleeper, she heaved herself out of the armchair and fumbled for the cordless phone.

It was Sloan Jones from the newspaper. He was a former student of hers, much as she hated to admit it. The rag he edited wasn't a glowing testament to her abilities as an English teacher. And she'd never in her wildest nightmares pictured Sloan in an English-related job as he stumbled through 10th grade English in her classroom. Nevertheless, everyone in town read the *Bradley Bugle* and it bore the hallmark of a successful newspaper: it was filled with local and regional advertisers. Red had arranged for his mother to have a column for the paper—he'd been trying to keep her busy, as usual. Recently, Sloan had treated her more as an investigative reporter, considering her closeness to Red...and, actually, to murder in general. It was the story she planned for his paper that provided her the most legitimate excuse for getting involved with the case.

"Mrs. Clover," Sloan said in his carefully respectful voice, "I was wondering what you might know about this murder at the hair salon." Myrtle smiled. Sloan always sounded like he was worried Myrtle was going to put him in afterschool detention. "Do you get your hair done there? Or maybe Red has talked about the case a little? I've got nothing, so I thought I'd check in with you." He patted his balding head ruefully. "And I don't have to get my hair cut too often."

"Now Sloan, you weren't going to cut me out of the story, were you? Because I don't want to just be one of your sources—I want to write the whole article."

"Of course, Mrs. Clover! No, I wouldn't cut you out of a story, you know that. I just didn't know if you *wanted* the story. Or if you even knew anything about it. Because you might get your hair done at the Cut-Ups, for all I know."

"No, I've gone to the Beauty Box for years and years. I *do* have some very good information, I just need to get a little more before I write the story."

"Are you about to crack the case?" Sloan sounded suddenly very cheerful. The paper had sold extra copies when Myrtle had her investigative story after the last Bradley murder. The article had even made it on the AP wire.

"Welllll....just between you and me? Yes. But don't go telling anybody or you're going to blow it." Because Red would find out and shut her down pretty quickly. "But you could help me out, you know. Maybe you could share some of your thoughts about some of the suspects in the case."

Sloan sounded surprised. "Sure. I'm not sure how helpful I'll be, though. I don't think I even get around town as much as you do...I follow the same patterns every day."

One of those patterns, though, involved drinking after work. "I thought maybe you'd have some insights for me on Tammy, that's all. Like I said, she's done my hair for years, but I thought you might have seen a different side to her than I did."

Sloan sighed. "Tammy was a hot mess for the last five or six months. Always gossiping about folks. I wondered if she was even telling the truth. I got half my copy for the gossip page from Tammy."

"Did you see much of her?" Since they were both recreational drinkers, they had to have run into each other a lot.

"She was over at the bar and the ABC store a lot. I saw her the night she was murdered, too. She and Connor Walker were eating at the pizza parlor, and I'd popped by to pick up my take-out order. Tammy had a huge fight with Connor. He's a guy who usually keeps his temper, but he couldn't keep a lid on it that night."

"What happened?"

Myrtle could hear the groans of his wheeled chair as he shifted his considerable weight. "Tammy had obviously been drinking...a lot. Connor was talking to her in a real quiet voice to keep their conversation private. But Tammy was yelling back at him, repeating half of what he said. It sounded like he was breaking up with her. I guess he thought if he dumped her in a restaurant, she wouldn't make a big scene. Tammy didn't care about what people thought about her, though. She couldn't believe he wanted to break up with her. She was cussing him out, calling him names."

"Was Connor mad?" asked Myrtle.

"He kept his cool better than most men. He got quieter as she got louder. You could tell he was furious, though, because his face was red and his hands were shaking. Tammy threw her plate at him and he walked out."

"That was probably the best thing to do."

"Not as far as Tammy was concerned. She didn't like being walked away from. Being left there made her madder, and she kept throwing things until *she* was covered with food, too. Next thing I heard, she was dead."

Myrtle was quiet for a moment, thinking. "Did you tell all this to the police?"

"Several times. I told it to Red and to the state police, too. I guess Connor could have fumed a while, then gone back later to the Beauty Box to finish the argument after he'd thought up some good comebacks. He might not have planned anything, but killed her in the heat of the moment."

"What do you know about Dina?" asked Myrtle. "I've never really been able to figure her out."

Sloan said, "I knew her ex was a bad guy. He came to the bar a few times. Dina did right to get away from him. But Tammy wasn't much better, I don't think. Dina always looked like she was sort of scared of Tammy. I think Tammy shouted at her a lot."

"I think you're right," said Myrtle.

"Anyway, that's all I know, and it's not much." It sure wasn't. Most of that she'd already known.

"And Mrs. Clover? If you think of anything else you want to write a story about, or if you want to write something about the investigation so far, feel free. I really need more content for the next issue. Alma Jane ran off to Myrtle Beach without turning in her 'remember when' column and now the gardening column isn't ready because Sue Perry is sick."

"I'm sure that I'll be wrapping this case up soon, Sloan. It'll be a fantastic story, believe me. I'll solve the case before your deadline."

Chapter Eleven

It was most disappointing how efficient Elaine's new cleaner was. Myrtle's mind had clearly been poisoned by the indolent Puddin and her sluggish housekeeping. She'd expected that she and Jo would have a little chatting time while Jo stalled. Myrtle was *used* to stalling. What was truly baffling was Jo's highly-developed work ethic.

Myrtle drummed her fingers on the kitchen table as Jo energetically attacked the kitchen floor—on her hands and knees, no less. She'd tried to bring up a little conversation, but Jo was so focused on the task at hand that she either grunted a response or offered something monosyllabic in reply.

Jo didn't even glance up as Myrtle's cell phone rang. "Hello?" Myrtle demanded, unable to keep the irritation from her voice. "What?" It was Red.

Red growled into his phone, "Mama, your unit is so old that they've had to order a replacement part for it. And the warehouse that makes the part was out of stock." He sighed. "I don't suppose you want to just get a whole new system put in, do you?"

"With whose money? Retired schoolteachers don't have that kind of cash, Red. And I don't think small-town police chiefs do, either."

"That's for sure." His voice sounded tight. "I guess you'll be staying with us another night. They seem to think it could be shipped over tomorrow. Expedited."

"Believe me, I'm no happier about this than you are. I've got stuff I need to do at home." Myrtle hung up, muttering to herself.

To her surprise, Jo finally decided to talk. "You were just staying here short term, Miss Myrtle? I didn't know what the story was."

Myrtle sighed. "It's a short story. Broken a/c. Hot octogenarian. You know."

"We're going to have to get our unit replaced soon. I've got a repairman over almost every month. It keeps needing coolant added—I guess there's a leak in the lines somewhere." Jo asked in a kind voice, "You'll miss being over here, won't you? When your air is fixed? I bet you get lonely, living by yourself."

So Jo felt some pity for her. It was easy to see how she came up with that impression, since Myrtle had been following her from room to room, trying to have a conversation. It was the perfect way to take advantage of the situation.

"It does get lonely." Myrtle did her best to look sad but brave. "One of my biggest pleasures is just to sit and chat with people." Jo frowned a little and Myrtle realized she might be taking it a little too far. She hurriedly added, "Red and Elaine try to make time for me, of course, but Red is busy with work and Elaine has Jack." She shrugged.

Jo gave a quick glance at the kitchen clock, then pulled out a chair. She really was a nice woman. And nice was definitely easier to work with when you were trying to get information out of someone.

"Am I messing you up?" Myrtle asked. "You're heading off to Bootsie's after this, right?" She leaned in near Jo as if there were spies listening in. "By the way, doesn't Bootsie look disgraceful these days? She's trying to dress as if she were a teenager!" She clucked and shook her head.

Jo laughed. "She's going through a midlife crisis, I guess."

"Midlife? To what? Is she going to live until one-hundred and twenty?"

Now Jo really laughed. "She's not that old. Yet."

"I can't wrap my mind around what she's trying to do with her look," said Myrtle with indignation. "Wearing short skirts and tall boots and sleeveless blouses at her age?" She rolled her eyes. "It makes me half-think that she's got some sort of love interest."

Jo's gaze sharpened and Myrtle looked innocently back at her. "Mercy, it looks like *you* think she has some sort of love interest, too."

Jo studied her as if gauging the danger of gossiping with Myrtle. Myrtle did her very best to look as innocuous as possible. "Well, be sure not to say anything to anybody, but I've wondered. You know—because of the way she's dressing."

"Have you seen Bootsie out with anyone?"

Jo shook her head. "No ma'am, I sure haven't. But I've noticed something unusual in the last couple of months. Like you said, she started dressing different and wearing more makeup. After I get there, she'll be upstairs getting ready to go out, then heads out of the house right before lunch. She's always got tons of perfume on— and I get headaches when I smell floral scents."

"Did you ever ask her where she was going?"

Jo said, "The first time I did. That's because it wasn't her normal routine. So I asked her if she were going out for lunch with friends. And she turned bright red and started stuttering like she didn't know what to say. Then she rushed out the door." Jo shook her head. "I didn't ask her again. But it does make you wonder."

Yes, it did. It sounded like a little surveillance was in order.

THE SURVEILLANCE WAS going to take a little prep-work—and involved borrowing Miles' car again. Since he seemed to treat the car like it was his own child, it was going to take a little doing to get Miles on board. In the meantime, Prissy was the next suspect on Myrtle's list, and she decided to go pay a little visit to her.

Taking some children's books with her would probably make her mission more believable. Then she could ask Prissy's opinion of the books. She threw a few books from Jack's room into a canvas bag, then crossed the street to her house. There was a small box with some of Red's childhood books at the top shelf of the hall closet.

Minutes later, Myrtle carefully climbed Prissy's steep stairs, set down the bag of books on the porch and balanced with the cane while ringing the old-fashioned buzzer.

Prissy peered out the lacy curtains beside the front door. With reluctance, she opened the door. "I wish you'd just call, Miss Myrtle. I hate you climbing these steep stairs." She opened the door, motioning Myrtle inside.

"Stairs? Oh, they're no problem for me. I'm fit as a fiddle. I just thought I'd drop by real quick and get your opinion on the books I picked out to read to your preschoolers."

She sat down gingerly on the old settee in Prissy's living room and pulled out the books as Prissy rambled on, praising her devotion to literacy.

Something, though, was apparently wrong. Prissy was staring at the books that Myrtle had brought.

"It's sweet of you to think of the children. They'll love to have you read to them. But..." Prissy sighed. "These books are a little too advanced for the preschoolers. I don't think the three and four-year-olds will grasp *Robinson Crusoe* or...*Crime and Punishment*."

Prissy continued rummaging through the bag. "And the board books must be some of Jack's old books." She held up *Baby's Busy Day*. Myrtle winced. She should have checked those books before she left. Prissy must think she's senile.

Prissy continued prattling. "I wouldn't expect you to have children's books lying around, Myrtle. Why don't you run by the library? The children's librarian—remember Miss Hatch?—will probably be happy to point you in the right direction."

Myrtle suffered through Prissy's high-volume monologue for several minutes, nodding at what she hoped were appropriate times. Growing impatient, she slumped in her chair, fanned herself and waited for Prissy to realize something was wrong. When Prissy continued her adulation of the benevolent Miss Hatch, Myrtle clutched her head and gave a melodramatic moan.

Prissy blinked at her as Myrtle gasped, "So sorry, Prissy. Your steep steps unsettled me more than I thought. Room...spinning. Fix me a drink?"

Prissy started clucking again, clicking her dentures and casting anxious looks at Myrtle before scurrying to the kitchen. In the meantime, Myrtle spryly hopped up and hustled to the back bedroom.

A sappy screensaver of birds flying under a rainbow covered the computer monitor. Myrtle jiggled the mouse and a word processing program came up. Myrtle gaped at the erotic writing on the screen. No flowery Regency prose here, only descriptive passages of a passionate love scene. And, judging from the stacks of nearby paperbacks, all by Tessa Rose; she'd written quite a number of them.

Myrtle high-tailed it back to her chair to resume her medical episode. She was just in time, as Prissy hurried in with a glass and a small pitcher of ice water on a small tray.

She drank a little of her water as Prissy fussed around her. "Let me get a cool washcloth for you. You've just lost all of your color!" Prissy walked to the back of the house, babbling as she went, until she suddenly went quiet. Myrtle froze. Had the screensaver cut back on, or did Prissy have it set on a delay? Prissy finally returned with the washcloth and a shrewd look on her face.

Myrtle took the washcloth and held it against her forehead as she gave a weak smile. "I feel much better now. Thanks for all your help. I really should go to the doctor and find out what's causing these spells! Um...let's see. Where were we? Oh yes. So, what day will be best to read to the children?"

Tersely, Prissy said, "I'll have to give you a call. I'm not really sure right now what the schedule looks like for next week." Myrtle drained her water and rose.

"Well, thanks again. I should probably go." She grabbed her cane and hefted the heavy bag of books. Prissy opened the front door for her and Myrtle stood at the top of the stairs before turning to ask Prissy if the children had a favorite book for her to ask for at the library.

Myrtle was never able to fully remember what happened next. It all seemed to take place at once: Prissy's surprisingly strong hand on her arm, Myrtle's loss of balance, her stumble, and the horrible sensation of falling.

Chapter Twelve

Apparently a previously dormant and uninvolved guardian angel miraculously steadied Myrtle and kept her from pitching head-long down the staircase.

This time she wasn't faking her weakness when she sank down onto the top step of the porch. Prissy gasped, "You nearly met your Maker!"

"And you were trying to help Him make my acquaintance," panted Myrtle. "You shoved me!"

Prissy's face was white. "Of *course* not. I was trying to steady you. You wobbled before you fell forward. Naturally, I wasn't in the right position to *stop* your fall..."

"Naturally." Waving aside Prissy's invitation to come back inside to rest, Myrtle carefully maneuvered down the stairs and through the tidy yard to the street. Feeling every one of her eighty-odd years, Myrtle trudged back to Red's house where she had her first afternoon nap in years.

Myrtle didn't feel in a very chatty mood at supper. Or a hungry one, she thought as she pushed her food around on her plate.

Red raised his eyebrows. "Not interested in shrimp and grits, Mama? I know that's one of your favorite meals." Myrtle looked at him balefully and he continued, "Okay, spill it. What's happened?"

She was just deciding that she could give him a taste of his own medicine and clam up, when she realized that this was the perfect way to bring up the case in a non-pushy, Red-repellant way. So Myrtle reluctantly told Red and Elaine about her afternoon with Prissy and its exciting climax where she nearly broke her neck on Prissy's front stairs.

"Miss Prissy tried to *push* you down the stairs?" Red's eyes were huge.

"You're making it sound ridiculous. But I'm sure I felt her bony hand on me, and it wasn't trying to steady me. I steadied myself."

"So, what you're saying, Mama, is that you think Prissy killed Tammy by shoving her down the stairs, and she was going to shove *you* down the stairs, too? Don't you think that sounds a little crazy, if she was trying to distance herself from the first crime? And all because of some dirty books?"

"I think shoving two victims down steep staircases is *exactly* what Prissy would do. She's not the most creative person around," answered Myrtle.

"Apparently Prissy is *very* creative. After all, she's writing erotic fantasies and making all that content up. Unless she's somehow living a secret life and writing from her own experiences."

Myrtle shuddered. "I guess she's more creative than I gave her credit for. Maybe she didn't mean for me to fall down the stairs, just to shake me up a little and give me a warning."

Elaine frowned as she absentmindedly scrubbed some grits off Jack's face. "I don't totally understand why Miss Prissy is so desperate to hide these books. She'd be a local celebrity if the word got out."

"Not likely," said Myrtle. "Remember, this is a small Southern town. The preschool mommies would never be able to look her in the eye again. Maybe she wouldn't feel comfortable at the program anymore, with parents giggling over her all the time. I don't know how Tammy found out about the books, but it's obvious she knew about them. Prissy could've gone over to the Beauty Box later that night and pleaded with Tammy to keep quiet. But then things could have gotten out of hand."

Red shook his head. "I just don't see it, Mama. Remember, the killer wore gloves. That shows premeditation, not a crime committed in the heat of an argument. And I still don't know how Tammy could have known about the books."

Myrtle glared at him. "Maybe she reads erotic romance and saw something that made her realize Prissy was the author. Actually, Prissy probably *told* her about the books. Tammy frequently belittled Prissy, so maybe Prissy burst out one day that she was a published author. Who knows? And maybe Prissy still wears driving gloves. She's so prim that I'd believe it. Or maybe it was premeditated after all. If she's wicked enough to try to shove innocent ladies down staircases, she's probably capable of anything."

Red frowned at her. "I'm still having trouble with this shoving thing."

"Prissy shoved me." Myrtle spoke slowly, in case Red was having cognitive trouble.

"Prissy did."

"Yes."

"Ninety-five pound Prissy." Red tilted his head at his mother.

"Your point being?"

"Ninety-five pound cadaverous Prissy pushed strapping, one-hundred and— "

"Never mind! I'm an old woman, Red, growing feebler every day."

Red looked doubtful.

Elaine spoke up, "Are you going to pull Miss Prissy in for questioning? These books show that she had a motive to kill Tammy. She wanted to keep her secret."

"This doesn't do anything but give the police a line of questioning. Now listen," he said as both Elaine and Myrtle butted in, "Listen, y'all! There's no hard evidence. There's nothing linking Miss Prissy to the homicide. But next time we talk to her, I can ask questions about her books…I'll say that we have a source that informs us that she has this secret series. We'll see what Lieutenant Perkins and I can find out."

"That doesn't sound promising. In fact, it sounds like my boring, exhausting, and dangerous afternoon tea with Prissy Daniels was all for nothing," said Myrtle with disgust.

"I wouldn't say that," replied Red. "It's shown us what her motive might have been." He grinned. "And those little preschoolers sure will love your stories, Mama."

It was never fun to wake up at night realizing you'd forgotten something. And that night, Myrtle sat up straight in bed, gasping. The cat! Oh no. Poor Pasha would be wondering where her food and water were. She *was* a feral cat, but she'd gotten used to being spoiled.

Myrtle grabbed her robe and slippers, her cane, and her keys. This time she really would have to be quiet. If Red caught her outside again in the middle of the night, he'd probably clamp on one of those ankle bracelets they put on criminals on house arrest.

She slipped out the front door, locking it behind her, and hurried across the street, letting herself in the front door. Myrtle found some cat food in the kitchen and put it outside in the backyard with a big bowl of water. She heard a rustling in her bushes and out ran Pasha, looking *very* glad to see her. There was something very rewarding in that.

She rubbed Pasha for a few minutes, talking to her in a soft voice, before walking back into the house again. Myrtle was just walking to the back door when she saw with horror that the painting was back on her mantel. When had Miles returned it? How had he gotten in?

Myrtle snatched the painting off her mantel. It was time to return the favor. And she just *happened* to still have a set of keys to Miles' house from when she housesat for him.

Miles' back door made all kinds of squeaks and groans. She froze, but he never appeared. She took the painting and slid it in the narrow space between his refrigerator and counter. There. That should take a while for him to find it.

The doorbell rang and Red raised his eyebrows. "Kind of early, isn't it?" he muttered. He looked out the door. "It's Miles," he told her before he pulled open the door.

"Sorry if it's early," said Miles, carrying a bag with one hand and pushing his steel framed glasses up his nose with the other. "Well, I *knew* Myrtle would be up, and Red, I figured you'd be about to head off to the station. But Jack and Elaine..."

"Elaine is already at the gym doing a yoga class or something," said Red, taking a last bite of his English muffin and wiping his mouth off with a napkin. "And Jack is...well, he's really quiet. Which probably means he's up there coloring on his wall with a Sharpie or something. I'll check on him before I head out," he said, hurrying off. "Help yourself to some coffee, Miles."

"You know," said Miles in a thoughtful voice, "I had terrible nightmares last night."

"Did you, Miles? I'm sorry to hear that," said Myrtle. She spread some butter on a muffin.

Miles poured himself a cup of coffee. "Yes. It was almost as if there was some horrible piece of artwork that was poisoning my dreams just by its very presence in my house."

Myrtle took a bite of the muffin and shrugged.

"Then," said Miles, speaking very precisely, "I discovered that there *was* a horrible piece of artwork in my house."

"How very observant of you. Interestingly enough, I made the same discovery myself recently."

"Yes. Well, while I was over getting your mail, I dropped the painting off for you to enjoy it for a while. I'm supposed to be having houseguests shortly—some family coming through town to visit. I think it might be best if the painting stays at your house for a while. Especially considering that you're not even there, yourself."

"Fine. I guess. Well, thanks for the mail, anyway," said Myrtle, taking the small stack from him. "You know, I used to wait for the mailman every day because I actually had *real* mail. Now it's just a few bills or statements or maybe a little junk mail. That's probably why I forgot to get it—it's just not interesting anymore."

Miles pointed at one envelope. "This one looks a little interesting. Or at least it doesn't look like junk mail."

"It might be something for my helpful hints column," said Myrtle with a puffy sigh. "I keep thinking I'm done with that stupid column now that I'm an investigative reporter for the *Bugle*. But Sloan keeps yanking me back into it because people still send tips and read the thing. I might end up writing that column from the grave."

She opened the envelope and her breath went out in a hiss between her teeth. "Holy moly."

"What is it?" Miles moved next to her.

"It's a tip all right." She showed him the paper, which had letters cut out from a newspaper to form words that said "Here's a tip for you—watch your back!"

Miles looked at the paper solemnly. "Myrtle, it looks like it's time you backed off."

"Oh, I don't know, Miles. As far as warnings go, this one isn't all that harsh."

"You don't think a threatening letter should be taken seriously?" Miles thoughtfully studied the paper again.

"Not at all. Not compared to being pushed down the stairs, anyway."

"*What?*"

So Myrtle had to fill him in, which she did while she poured them both some more coffee. Miles seemed to share Red's point of view of Miss Prissy as evildoer. "Really?" he asked in a doubtful voice. "I just somehow don't see Prissy flinging people down stairs."

Myrtle was about to hotly debate this point when Red hurried back in again. "Okay, all's fine. He covered his room with toilet paper, but that's not as bad as other stuff he could have done." He looked at the pile of mail on the kitchen table. "What's that?"

Myrtle showed him the letter. "Are you going to check it for fingerprints?"

Red answered, "Paper doesn't usually hold fingerprints. I'll show it to the forensic guys, but I doubt anything will turn up. Besides, it might not have even come from the killer. It's not like I can pin a murder on whoever sent this out."

"There's got to be something you can find out about it. With all the forensics stuff the state police has?"

Red shook his head. "Not really, Mama. The message was glued on standard printer paper, and this is just a plain business envelope. Anybody in town could have picked them up at the drugstore. The newspaper was probably the *Bradley Bugle*, which everyone gets. It's not like it's going to be cut from the *New York Times*, and we just have to find out who subscribes. Nothing in life is that easy."

"You can't look for cut up newspaper in people's trash or see if the suspects have this same type of paper or envelopes?"

"I can't search every house in town, Mama. I can't search *any* houses unless I have probable cause, which I don't. This isn't even technically a threatening letter. It doesn't threaten bodily harm or blackmail."

Miles said, "Whoever sent it sure didn't mail it with goodwill, though. It was unsolicited in her mailbox."

"So is all the junk mail we get. Look, I'll try my best, but don't get your hopes up." Red grabbed his car keys, mumbled out a goodbye and left.

Miles and Myrtle moved into the living room where Jack was now playing with some toy trucks. "You know, Miles, I must be getting close enough to scare somebody."

"Exactly why you should quit. Let Red and the state police do their jobs."

"I'm letting them do their jobs. Actually, I'm *helping* them do their jobs by finding leads for them. I ought to be on their payroll," said Myrtle.

"I think you ought to back off. You're not paying any attention to this warning."

Myrtle glanced down at the note again. "Prissy is the first person who comes to mind."

"You're developing a Prissy complex. It could be any of the suspects."

"I somehow don't see Connor smearing newspaper cut-outs with glue sticks. It just seems like a sort of girly thing to do," said Myrtle.

"He could have done it," argued Miles. "It would have been a way to scare you off the case without really *hurting* you."

"I wish I knew what Tammy had on the other suspects. Judging from Prissy's secret, she must have had something juicy on them. Let's brainstorm."

Miles looked a little out of his depth.

"Oh, come on, Miles! You've got some imagination deep down inside you somewhere. You *must* have some, if you had a career as an architect."

"Engineer," he said through gritted teeth.

"Whatever. Now, if I were a writer for my soap opera, I'd come up with tons of possibilities."

"Maybe Bo is a CIA agent, worried about having his cover blown. The diner could just be a front," suggested Miles hesitantly.

"How fanciful of you, Miles! Yes, that's exactly the kind of brainstorming I mean. Except, of course, that's completely wrong. Bo has never stepped foot out of this town his whole life. Anyway, he has an alibi."

"Okay. Hmm. Bootsie is actually a closet PETA operative. Her furs are fakes and she spends her lunch hours rescuing animals from cosmetics testing." Miles looked smug as Myrtle clapped.

"I've got one. Prissy is a man," said Myrtle, waving her finger at Miles.

"How about this: Connor isn't really Agnes' son; she snatched him from a stroller during a trip to Alabama."

They both burst out laughing. Wiping the tears from her eyes, Myrtle said, "Ok, that was good for a giggle. But who knows? In this town, it *could* be true. I'm going to go out later when Elaine gets back and investigate some more. I'll call you later to check back in."

WHEN ELAINE CAME IN from the gym, she saw Myrtle staring blankly at *The Price is Right* while she and Jack munched on animal crackers. Myrtle sighed. "You know, it's way too easy to turn into a couch potato here. At home I'd find stuff to do. And, by the way, it looks like I'll be back in there by this evening—the part they ordered came in and they installed it. I'm just waiting for the house to cool back down again."

Elaine's face was carefully and pleasantly neutral at the news that her mother-in-law would be packing up and heading home.

Myrtle said, "I know you just came in, but do you want to go back out again? Jack and I are bored silly. I thought maybe we could go shopping at the department store or something."

"Sure. I just need to shower and change real quick. Did you need to shop for something in particular?"

"I could use a new dress. At my age, people really start flaking out. Especially in this town, with all the murders. I need to update my funeral wardrobe."

"Okay, if that's what you really need. But I wish you'd get your mind out of the casket."

Brogan's department store carried everything from girdles to gadgets and games. Myrtle changed, too, because whenever you went to Brogan's, you were bound to run into someone you knew. It was housed in an ancient brick two-story building. The management treasured anachronisms such as the regal elevator-door opener.

Elaine and Myrtle had just started shopping when they spotted a familiar face. It was a familiar *face*, but the hair above the face wasn't familiar at all. Myrtle yanked Elaine's sleeve and hissed, "Is that Agnes Walker?"

Elaine stood on tiptoe, peering over several racks of clothes. "With the bright blue hair? No, it couldn't be."

It was. A glum Agnes turned when they called her. She was shopping for headscarves and broke in before Myrtle could begin her interrogation. "I know, it's dreadful. I sometimes get a faint blue tint for my gray, but I never asked to look like a *blueberry*. That Dina! She offered to fix it at the shop when I was so horrified, but I told her to keep her hands off it! I'm going to have to schedule an appointment with Kat."

Myrtle said, "I didn't think Dina knew how to color hair."

Agnes snorted, "Well, obviously she doesn't. She claims she took a course at the tech-school a few months ago."

Agnes patted her head gingerly as Elaine wandered off to a sales rack with Jack. "I've been feeling a little sorry for Dina since her breakdown in the salon, and I foolishly offered her the chance to practice on my head."

"Altruism always causes trouble."

"You *would* say that," said Agnes. "As soon as Dina walked out of the room to get the color ready, Kat warned me. She said that she'd offered herself as a guinea pig to Dina one night and Dina had chickened out. To her, that meant she's not ready to color hair." Agnes sighed. "I should have known disaster was imminent. How could anyone worry about messing up *Kat's* hair? It's pink, for crying out loud!"

"I don't really see a future for Dina in hair," mulled Myrtle. "She's gotten very involved with that women's shelter lately. I guess with Tammy out of the way, Dina's getting a sense of who she is now."

Agnes said, "Myrtle, I'm surprised at that new-age-speak, 'who she is.' She's Dina Peters with an unfortunate penchant for screwing up, that's who she is."

"You should get a chance to counsel her on who she is pretty soon. She's been going door to door collecting for that shelter," said Myrtle.

"Counseling is exactly what she needs. And she needs to be relieved of her chemicals."

Myrtle couldn't smother a snicker at Agnes' droll expression. Elaine returned with a pretty scarf. "This one looks like you, Miss Agnes."

"It's perfect, Elaine, and you're a sweet girl. Your Red lucked out, Myrtle. I wish Connor could settle down with a nice girl."

Here it comes. The agonizing over Connor's budding involvement with Kat. But Agnes' mind was occupied as she fumbled in her voluminous pocketbook for an equally large billfold. "Better run and buy this to cover my blue locks. Take care." She left without looking back.

Elaine stared after her. "Well. That was abrupt, wasn't it?" Turning back to Myrtle, she asked, "What do you think about these dresses? The green one is more on sale than the blue one, but I could dress the green one up or dress it down..."

Myrtle had the enviable talent of appearing to listen attentively while her thoughts drifted. She nodded encouragingly at Elaine and even managed to choose her favorite dress when Myrtle gathered she was being asked her opinion. But her mind worked full-speed on Agnes. Jack dropped Dirty Doggy and Myrtle absently gave it back to him. Was Agnes' warning the other day prompted by her concern over Connor's involvement? Could Connor have killed Tammy in an impulsive moment? If Agnes knew something, she'd cover up for him at all cost.

What about Agnes herself? The thought made Myrtle shift uncomfortably. But it seemed like a possibility. Maybe she couldn't stand the thought of his dating or marrying Tammy. Agnes was old but strong and could easily have pushed Tammy down the stairs. Could she have plunged the scissors in Tammy's back, though? Probably. If she thought she was protecting Connor.

"What do you think of this? I found it while I was looking for the scarf for Agnes." Elaine held up a prissy-looking one piece gingham romper with a Peter Pan collar.

"I think he'll look like Raggedy Andy, Elaine." She was rewarded by seeing her grandson beam at her with relief as his mother put the romper back on the rack. Another Good Deed.

Chapter Thirteen

Elaine helped Myrtle pack up her bags and carry them to her house, which was nicely cool. Actually, Elaine said it was a little on the chilly side, but Myrtle didn't notice. She was still trying to figure out who Bootsie was sneaking around with. As soon as Elaine left, Myrtle picked up the phone. "Miles? Could you come over for a minute? No, to my house...the air is fixed."

Miles had barely settled himself into her living room sofa when Myrtle launched in. "Miles, I need you to flirt with Bootsie and squeeze some information out of her."

Miles stared at her coldly. "I won't. Besides, I'm too old for Bootsie."

"But she's nearly *your age*!"

"That's what I mean. I'm too old for her," said Miles.

Myrtle stared at him. "You know something, don't you?"

"I might have seen her leaving a tryst," he said in a grudging voice. "I was driving by the motel, so I couldn't identify the person. But I got the impression he was really young."

Myrtle asked, "When was this? You couldn't have told me this earlier?"

"Earlier it just would have been gossip. And now I'm not sure it's more than that, either. But now that I've thought of it, I guess I should tell Red or Lieutenant Perkins what I saw. Then they can decide if it's relevant or not."

"Now, Miles, let's not be hasty. There's no point in telling the police anything about Bootsie's little indiscretion. You're right—it's probably not important at all. Just in case, though, you and I should go check it out."

"How are you planning to do that?" asked Miles, his tone very polite.

"We'll have a stakeout. Complete with doughnuts. I'll buy them. We were going to do surveillance anyway, and it sure is a lot easier now that we know where Bootsie has been going for her tryst."

"Myrtle, I really don't want to hang out in a second-rate motel all day, waiting for a rendezvous that might not even happen."

"No, no, it'll be fine. You've given me the place, and Jo has given me the time that Bootsie leaves for her assignations. It's going to be an easy-peasy stakeout. So you could pick me up tomorrow before lunch."

Miles nodded glumly.

"Oh. And, by the way, I need to borrow your car."

Miles closed his eyes, looking pained. "Please don't tell me you're going off on another joyride in the country. Last time, it took me forever to get all the mud off my car."

"No joyrides. I just need to go visit my...spiritual advisor."

Miles looked ridiculous with his mouth hanging open like a fish. Myrtle felt a flash of irritation, which she squashed since she hadn't gotten the car yet. "Plenty of people have them, Miles."

"So, you're going to see a *minister*? He's giving you Biblically-based guidance?"

Miles' eyes were just a little too widely innocent. She was sure he knew exactly what she was referring to, but was trying to embarrass her. He should know that most elderly ladies were beyond embarrassment. "No," she gritted through her teeth. "I mean a seer. A clairvoyant. A psychic."

Miles grinned at her. "You're not seeing that Madam Zora person off the old highway, are you? The same place that sells tires and boiled peanuts? She's got to be a total quack."

"It's *not* tires; it's hubcaps. And I think they stopped selling boiled peanuts a long time ago."

Miles frowned thoughtfully. "You're not at all gullible, though. You don't mean—"

"That she has the sight? Yes, that's exactly what I mean. She's legit."

"You mean she can really predict the future?" Miles squinted skeptically.

"She apparently has a gift." Myrtle shrugged as if psychic gifts were something one encountered every day.

"Maybe I'd like to go with you then," said Miles slowly. "When are you heading over there?"

"Right now."

"Now?" Miles glanced at his watch. "But I'm about to have to wait around for my plumber to come over. Can't you go later?"

"Not in the interest of justice, Miles, no. I'm on a timetable here. What if the killer strikes again? Don't worry; I'll fill you in on all the details when I get back."

THE RIDE OUT TO THE shack that Wanda (Madam Zora) shared with her brother was a little ways out of town. Myrtle always knew she was getting closer because the church signs became more and more ominous as she approached. They started out with a heartfelt *Jesus loves you*, before moving on to the slightly more pointed *Forbidden fruit creates many jams.* By the time she finally puttered up to the turnoff for Wanda's house, the last sign said *Choose the bread of life or you are toast.*

The small house where Crazy Dan and Wanda lived was entirely covered with hubcaps. The pair supposedly made their living from selling hubcaps, bait, and psychic readings. Myrtle had a feeling they probably received a little government help in the form of Social Security or disability pay, too.

Myrtle carefully maneuvered across the gravel of the driveway to the house and rapped her cane on the hubcaps. She noticed Wanda had a new sign duct taped to the metal: *Madam Zora. Sykick. Tarro Card reeding.* Crazy Dan poked his grizzled head out the door, a scowl on his leathery, stubble-covered features. "You again!"

"Hello to you, too, *Crazy* Dan," said Myrtle pointedly. "It's been months since I've been here. I'm not here to visit you, anyway. I want to see your sister."

Still looking her in the eye, he hollered, "Wander...uh, Madam Zora! You gotta for-toon to tell!" With that, the wizened, dirty man disappeared into the dark recesses of his small house.

If Myrtle hadn't met Wanda before, she'd have thought that Crazy Dan had just run into the back, put women's clothes on, and joined her again. Like her brother, she was skin and bones, with nicotine-stained hands and five or six teeth missing. She seemed surprised to see Myrtle—and a little unsettled. "You always come back," she muttered. She sadly added, "You come back, I warn you, and you never listen."

"I listen!" protested Myrtle. She just didn't *heed* it. She listened the whole time.

Wanda sucked in a deep, sustaining breath through her ruined lungs and grabbed Myrtle's hand as if it were a hot potato. "No, no, no," said Myrtle. "I don't want my palm read this time. I want you to do the tarot cards. I want to hear your thoughts on what's going on in my life."

Wanda's expression said that she really didn't want to delve too far into the nether regions of Myrtle's life. Grumbling, she yanked out a drawer and pulled out a disreputable looking deck of cards.

She slouched over to a rickety table, motioning Myrtle to follow her. She slapped the cards onto the table and examined them. "There's a man," she said. "He is close to you."

"Yes, yes," said Myrtle waving her hand in a circular motion. "Probably Red. What else?"

"He will help you."

"Hmm. Not Red then. Must be Miles. Okay, so Miles will help me. What's next?" This reading was not particularly helpful so far. "Can we use your crystal ball? I think we get better results with it."

Madam Zora looked balefully at her as she snatched the crystal ball off a nearby table. Rubbing the ball for effect, she intoned, "There's a woman. She's been hurt. Very deeply."

Myrtle rolled her eyes. "I'll say. She's dead." Money down the drain.

"Not dead. But dead inside."

That could apply to any number of women. Tammy hurt Kat, Prissy, Bootsie, Dina, and Agnes, too.

Wanda squinted at the dusty ball. "There's another woman. She's..." Wanda frowned. "Goin' on a trip." She seemed to sense Myrtle's irritation and said in a grand voice, "But there is death nearby."

Myrtle's head hurt. This reading was a total let-down for details.

"Can you see the woman, Wanda? Because it seems to me that if you can tell she's going on a trip, you ought to at least make out whether it's an old woman or a tall one or something."

"Madam Zora never sees faces," croaked Wanda. "I just see suitcases."

"How helpful," gritted Myrtle between her teeth. She fumbled for her cane. "You know, I just remembered there's something I need to do. I better go." With her left hand she fumbled in her pocketbook until she pulled out two tens. She showed Wanda one of them, then stuffed it back in her purse. "Ten dollars now, and ten dollars if the faces or other details ever get in focus."

Wanda nodded. Then she gave a resigned sigh and said, "Cards say *yer* in danger, too. Not that you care. Yer always in danger."

"Yes, well, that's fine. I don't know how you even know it's me that's in danger, since you don't see details." Myrtle sniffed. "Take care, Wanda."

She was almost to Miles' car when she heard the door screeching open behind her and quickly turned around. "Yes? Did you see something else, Wanda?" She clutched her pocketbook tight in her excitement at further revelations.

"Could you "like" me on Facebook?" Wanda leaned against the doorframe as if needing its help to stand up.

Myrtle stared at her. "Facebook? You're on Facebook? You have a *computer*?"

Wanda shook her head. "No computer. My cuzzin put me on the Facebook, though. Git lots of bizness that way."

Myrtle was accelerating to a regal thirty-five miles an hour when suddenly the car made a clunking noise, the check engine light came on, and she realized the accelerator was as good as useless. After some choice words, she stopped on the side of the road and fumbled for her cell phone. "Miles, your car is broken."

"Broken! What do you mean? Did you have a wreck?"

Myrtle said, "Of course not. But you could have told me it was broken."

"But it wasn't!"

"I'm going to need you to come and get me," said Myrtle.

"Impossible. You're in my car."

"Oh, right. Well. Okay, I'll call Red." This wasn't good. He'd wonder what she was doing out in the boonies in Miles' car. And he wasn't, for some reason, all that thrilled with her driving anymore. Who knew why?

Red arrived with Miles, who stayed with his car to wait for the tow truck. The drive back home was swift.

"Aren't you driving a little fast? I think we just passed a speeding bullet."

"Who's going to pull me over?" demanded Red.

Being a police chief had its perks.

"Although I don't know for the life of me what you're doing out here in the country."

Myrtle said, "I was proud of my renewed license, and I wanted to get in some practice time behind the wheel. That's all."

They seemed to really be driving at a fair clip. Myrtle clutched the door of the car in an obvious manner.

"Just chill out, Mama. I'm not even going that fast. Although, compared to the way you putter around, I guess I am."

"Sharper than a serpent's tooth...."

"I'm not a thankless child and you're not King Lear."

His level tones only infuriated Myrtle more. "I'm writing you and your bad attitude out of my will."

"Fine. All your worldly riches—or lack of them—won't change things a bit."

Myrtle ground her teeth. "Just so you know, I have plenty of worldly riches."

"A widowed schoolteacher?"

"You've been really overstepping your boundaries," she grumbled.

"And the retributive literature assignment?" grinned Red. Most of his childhood punishments involved Myrtle's forcing him to read and be tested on the driest, most arcane texts. This somehow hadn't killed his lifelong love of reading.

Myrtle considered. "All the chapters in *Moby Dick* that pertain to whale lines, darts, harpoons and general whale anatomy. Read them twelve times consecutively. Testing will be essay-style." She gave a hint of a smile.

They drove in silence for a moment, then Myrtle said, "How'd you find time to run out here and rescue me with a murder investigation going on?"

"The state police are doing most of the work right now. Although I still have plenty, believe me," said Red in a sour voice.

"What's happening with the case?"

He sighed. "Same as any other murder case, I guess. It's just that I'm not usually working murder cases. But Perkins hasn't solved Tammy's murder either, so I shouldn't feel bad that I haven't."

"What've they found out?"

"Nothing much. Mostly what you already know. Someone wearing gloves handled the murder weapon. The door to the Beauty Box wasn't locked or broken into; somebody just walked right in. There were no signs of a struggle. Tammy had her back to the killer, who stabbed her and pushed her down the stairs. No one heard or saw anything. The main suspects have no alibis and DNA from half the town was present in the salon."

Myrtle snorted. "No one saw anything? In this snoopy town? I think people know more than they want to let on. Or maybe they don't *know* that they know something."

Red pulled up into Myrtle's driveway. "Oh, since you're here," she ignored Red's groan, "could you grab the basket I put together for the women's shelter? Then you can drive me by the Beauty Box. I just can't hold my cane and the basket at the same time." She sounded as pitiful as she could. It was a good opportunity to try to talk to Dina Peters, too.

Red said, "I guess I have some time. Sure. Dina will be sorry to see me coming though; she does a frightened bunny act anytime I show up."

"Well, you're investigating her, after all. How do the others act?" asked Myrtle.

"About how you'd expect. Bootsie Davenport puts on a "lady of the manor" act with us. Kat Roberts is belligerent. Strange-looking girl, there. Let's see—Agnes Walker is courteous, but not helpful. Connor's defensive. And when we interview Prissy Daniels, I pack smelling salts in my pocket."

"Prissy couldn't be that bad," scoffed Myrtle.

Red looked thoughtful. "She might be faking it. I'd swear she's even tougher than Kat." He went in for the basket.

It occurred to Myrtle that there was something else that needed to be delivered. Really, Miles was being completely absurd about the painting. He always complained that his out-of-town guests would stay too long anyway. He only had the one bedroom, so when he had guests, he slept on a rollaway bed in his small office. She'd probably be doing him a good deed by leaving the painting for his guests to see it.

She hurried inside and grabbed the painting and Miles' house key. Since Miles was safely away, she quickly let herself in, put the painting against the bedroom wall, and hurried out. The snatches of the hymn wafted through her head. Yes, this painting could be responsible for Miles getting rid of his company in a timely fashion.

DINA WAS DELIGHTED to see them. Or to see Myrtle's donations, at least. Dina raved about the progress she and other volunteers had made at the shelter.

"And," she added, smiling shyly at Myrtle, "thanks for making me put the donation jar in Bo's diner. We've gotten so much money from people's spare change."

"Everybody in town goes to that diner, and it's the perfect way to get contributions," said Myrtle.

Red broke in. "Dina, while I'm here, did you remember anything else from the night of the murder?" Dina pushed up her big glasses anxiously to get a better look at Red. "Sorry to bring it up again, but the investigation is still going on, and your memories of that night aren't getting any fresher," he explained.

Gone was the self-assurance and enthusiasm present when Dina gushed over the shelter. She spluttered for a second before answering, "I don't think I came up with anything else, Chief Clover. I mean—it was a very boring night."

Red raised an eyebrow. "Aside from the murder where you lived and worked, you mean?"

The sarcasm unsettled Dina. "I don't know what you want me to remember."

Red sighed and Myrtle bit back a smile. Getting information from Dina was like squeezing blood from a particularly unintelligent turnip. "Dina, I don't *want* you to come up with things to remember. I want you to try thinking of little details, maybe things that were different than usual. Things that didn't seem important at the time but that stand out more now."

Dina fidgeted with her frizzy hair, pulling the curls out, then letting them coil back again. "I'm sorry. I just don't know. Like I said, I ate supper by myself, since Tammy had gone out with Connor. I fell asleep with the TV on. When I woke up, it was two or three in the morning. I turned off the TV and went back to sleep."

"You didn't hear anything from the salon side of the duplex?" asked Red.

Dina shook her head miserably. "The walls are pretty thick, so sound doesn't travel much from the salon to my room. The television probably blocked out some of the noise, too."

"No shouting? No arguments? No bodies thumping down the stairs?" Red asked.

She thought for a minute, then shook her head. "I'm sorry," she repeated again. She looked like a puppy waiting for encouragement.

"It's okay, Dina. Let me know if you do think of something." As Red and Myrtle walked out of the Beauty Box, Red shook his head in bewilderment. "I don't see how that girl functions. I really don't."

Myrtle said, "I bet her mind is a big warehouse full of discarded information that might be worth something. She's a nice enough girl. She just spooks easily. I hear she's been an angel at this women's shelter."

"Maybe. But being an angel doesn't make her any more fun to be around. Remember your favorite Twain quote?" asked Red.

"You mean: *Go to Heaven for the climate, Hell for the company?* Yes, I know."

Red sighed. "She's as scatterbrained as ever or even worse. I saw her wandering the streets yesterday holding a pair of hair shears like she was Edward Scissorhands. Her elevator just doesn't make it to the top floor."

Myrtle laughed. "She tried to abduct Dirty Doggy the other day. Walked right out the door carrying it and I had to chase her down."

Red looked ill at the thought of losing Dirty Doggy. "Don't tell me things like that, Mama. It's too scary to even contemplate."

The next morning, Myrtle's phone rang bright and early. "Miss Myrtle? It's Prissy. I wasn't sure if you'd still be at Elaine's or back at your own house by now."

It never ceased to amaze Myrtle how fast news traveled in small towns. "Yes, I'm back at home."

"I called to give you a tip for your column."

"Oh, good, I've been hoping to get some more. Reminds me to check my mailbox, too. What've you got for me?"

"I once heard that if you break a wine cork, you can strain the wine into your goblet through a coffee filter."

It was a strange tip from a cardigan-wearing, herbal tea-drinking teetotaler. "Got it. Thanks. While I've got you on the phone, is it okay if I read to your preschool classes Monday?"

"Of course, Miss Myrtle, that would be great. Try to come around ten-thirty. Did you find a good book to share?"

"The children's librarian picked out a couple."

"I know the kids will love them. Thanks so much," gushed Prissy before ringing off.

Prissy really did have a Dr. Jekyll and Mr. Hyde personality. Or could she really be imagining her hostility and the shove?

The doorbell rang. It was Miles, looking rather grim, for some reason. "Come on in, Miles. I was just getting off the phone with the evil Prissy. I'm convinced she's looking for another opportunity to push me down a staircase. I'll have to watch my step at her blasted preschool."

"You're calling each other on the phone now?"

"She was just calling with a tip for the column. One other than for me to be careful on steep staircases. I guess I'll have to write the column soon—I've been focusing all my time on the investigative reporting. Which reminds me—when are you picking me up for the stakeout?"

"Picking you up in *what*?" Miles' voice was suddenly cold.

Myrtle frowned at him. "In your car, Miles."

"My car is having its transmission replaced, even as we speak. I'm not sure what you did to it to break it—"

"Absolutely nothing! I was just driving. And very sedately, too! Clearly you put me in a defective vehicle." Myrtle sighed. "This is terrible news, Miles! When will they fix your car so we can have our stakeout?"

"They say it'll be ready to be picked up early tomorrow morning. But Myrtle, really, do we have to know the identity of Bootsie's paramour?"

"We don't have to know his *identity* so much. It's more to confirm that the rumors are true. There's no motive for Bootsie to have murdered Tammy if she's just sneaking off every week to get Botox injections or something," said Myrtle.

"This isn't a project that really appeals to me."

"How about if I just *borrow* your car, then. You don't even have to go."

This idea apparently was even less appealing to Miles. They made plans to meet the next morning.

THE MOTEL NEAR THE interstate overpass was intended for exhausted drivers desperate for shelter. The inn's philosophy was apparently that the poor traveler would be too pooped to notice the worn carpet, thin 1970s-era bedspreads, and the particleboard furniture. A decrepit neon sign proclaimed "Motor Lodge." Only the 'r' remained lit up. A smaller sign under the neon one advertised "HBO" and "American-Owned." Myrtle couldn't imagine another country that would claim it.

Miles parked the car under a tree in a distant parking space of the nearly deserted lot. "Look, there's her car," said Miles, pointing to a cream-colored Caddy. She shook her head as she considered the dismal motel. "Not listed in the travel agents' honeymooner registry, is it?"

"Well, if you think about it, it's the perfect place. No one would look for her here, after all. I bet the staff is pretty discreet...she's probably their best customer. She won't run into anybody she knows from town, and it isn't on Judge Davenport's route to the courthouse. Inexpensive and convenient. Anonymous."

"With Bootsie's airs and graces and the Southern Belle act she subjects us to, it's hard to believe that she hangs out at cheap motels."

"Yes, she does have a 'to the manor born' act." Myrtle frowned. "Is it 'to the *manner* born' or 'to the *manor* born'? Both make sense, if you think about it? From *Hamlet*, but which word did Shakespeare use?"

Miles shrugged, used to Myrtle's metaphysical ramblings and non sequiturs. He pulled out the binoculars and handed them to Myrtle. "You want the first look at our quarry when she comes out?"

"You know, this is very exciting. We're like real private eyes. All we need is a camera with a zoom lens to make us official," said Myrtle.

"And a paying client," reminded Miles.

"I'm still kind of surprised that she's doing this. I guess it's the thrill of it all. She's had a boring life, after all. She's been stuck with Judge Davenport her whole life. Now she's middle-aged and he's old. And from the looks of it, he's going to be around for a while. I don't think she has a lot of fun."

"Hold on, there's somebody walking out one of the doors on the second floor," said Miles.

"Is it Bootsie?"

Miles took the binoculars back and peered through them. "I guess so. But she sure doesn't look like president of the Cotillion board in that get-up."

Myrtle snatched the binoculars away from him. She gaped at Bootsie in three-inch heels and a mini skirt heading quickly down the staircase and towards her Cadillac. "What's she thinking? Has she been pilfering clothes from Kat's closet? Let's see if we can see who her companion is."

Myrtle held her breath as she swung the lenses back in the direction of the motel room door. Sure enough, a youthful dark-haired man sauntered out. "Now who is *he*? He looks somewhat familiar..." She handed the binoculars back over to Miles.

"My yardman," said Miles, staring at the figure. "I bet he does the Davenports' lawn, too."

"You must have a better-looking yardman than I do," grumbled Myrtle. "The only good part about Dusty is that he's cheap. That's the whole reason I can't fire his wife, Puddin. They're a package deal and it's impossible to find a cheap yardman in this town."

As her friend went into the motel's office to return the keys, Bootsie appeared to be wriggling into a matronly dress in the front seat while juggling her cell phone. She started the Cadillac and pulled quickly out of the parking space. Myrtle and Miles ducked down low until the sound of the engine died away. "She wasn't even really looking around to make sure no one was watching," said Miles.

"She's probably been doing this for so long that she's getting care-less. Maybe she feels safe here."

They watched as the handsome young man left the motel's office and noisily used his remote to unlock a sporty black car. He was dressed casually, but expensively, in jeans and a polo shirt. Myrtle and Miles watched silently, their eyes following his car as it roared off. They didn't notice the large figure striding rapidly towards them.

Chapter Fourteen

Still watching through binoculars, Myrtle mused, "What on earth could his motivation be? It's easy to see why Bootsie's so crazy about him. But what's driving *him*?"

"Money," answered a dry voice from outside their rolled down windows. Myrtle and Miles jumped half a mile as Red's angry face appeared through Myrtle's window. They'd been so absorbed in their surveillance that the arrival of Red's police cruiser had gone completely unnoticed. "Hi, Mama," he said in a tight voice. "Miles. Thought I recognized the car. What the blazes are y'all doing out here?"

"Just following up on a lead for my *Bradley Bugle* story," answered Myrtle calmly. "We're on a stakeout. What are you doing out here?"

Red barely held his temper in check. "This is my beat. And I thought you were watching Jack today, Mama." He peered into Miles' backseat as if looking for a car seat and a red-headed toddler.

"Elaine didn't need me to look after Jack today, after all. You know I wouldn't bring him on a stakeout."

"On a stakeout," repeated Red in disbelief. "No, I wouldn't ordinarily place Jack at a stakeout. But I wouldn't put my mother there, either."

"You should be proud of us," said Myrtle firmly.

"Have you had a mild stroke? Why on earth should I be proud of you?"

"I followed leads to find out what was behind Bootsie's secretive behavior." Myrtle paused for a minute to give Red the opportunity to applaud her detective work, but continued talking when the adulation wasn't forthcoming. "So I asked Miles to drive me out here. It was *my* idea and *not* Miles'."

"Mama, it never occurred to me in a million years that this was Miles' brainchild."

"Anyway, we got to the bottom of Tammy's hold on Bootsie. She's seeing some young guy and obviously doesn't want her husband to find out. Otherwise, she'd lose the easy life she's been living." Then she frowned. "Wait a minute. How'd you know his motive was money—and how'd you know what we were talking about?"

"Because," replied Red in a world-weary voice, "I'm well aware of Mrs. Davenport's goings-on. I could've told you all about them."

Myrtle gaped at him and he continued, "She makes sure he has everything he needs to be comfortable. She gets a big allowance from the Judge, apparently."

"Wait a minute," said Myrtle. "Shouldn't you be arresting him for prostitution?"

Red snorted derisively. "I'd have to arrest Bootsie herself if I went by that standard. Her husband has basically been paying Bootsie for thirty years to stick around. I think it's more of a sugar mama relationship. But you're right—I'm sure that Bootsie doesn't want the Judge to know about it. Maybe he *sort* of knows what she's up to, but he would divorce her for sure if he were publicly humiliated."

"Myrtle," said Miles in a carefully patient tone, "I'm ready to grab some lunch. Can we get out of here and head for the diner or something?"

"I guess," said Myrtle, still a little irritated about the fact that Red already knew about Bootsie's affair. "Red, do you want to join us?" At least maybe she could try to find out what else he knew.

"No, I'm still on patrol. I'm going to have to grab a late lunch today. Then I've got to meet up with Lieutenant Perkins to do another interview."

Myrtle's radar instantly went up. "Connor Walker, maybe?"

"None of your business, Mama." Which only confirmed to Myrtle that she was right.

Customers still packed Bo's Diner when Miles and Myrtle arrived at one-thirty. When a booth freed up, they slid in on its vinyl seats. "Fried chicken plate looks good," mused Myrtle. A pink head entered her peripheral vision. Kat said, "Got some tips for your column, Miss Myrtle."

Myrtle blinked a little at the thought of Kat having any kind of home tips, but she plucked out a pen and paper from her large pocketbook. "Shoot."

Kat cleared her throat for effect. "After painting a room, put your leftover paint in an empty mustard or ketchup bottle to squeeze out and spread for touch-ups, later. Also, instead of using lemon juice to keep peeled apples and bananas from browning in the air, try pineapple juice. It adds a little something extra to the fruit besides keeping it pretty," said Kat.

Myrtle slid over and patted the booth next to her for Kat to sit down. "You do surprise me, Kat. I never would have pegged you for a painter or a cook. Got any other hidden talents? Horseback riding? Piloting planes?"

Kat laughed. "No, that's about it."

"Well, I'm proud of you. There aren't many people who've had the rough past that you've had who are able to turn things around and make their life better. Good for you!" said Myrtle, beaming.

"Thanks," said Kat. "Although I've had some pretty low moments here in Bradley, too, where I was wondering if I'd done the right thing to move near Tammy. But now it looks like it's all going to work out just fine."

Miles nodded. "For a while it must have seemed like Tammy was trying to undo all the progress you'd made. I hear she was really driving customers off. You probably wondered if the Beauty Box was going to survive."

"She was screwing up all *her* chances, and I thought she was going to try to take me down with her, just like my mom had done. I couldn't let that happen to me again," said Kat.

When Myrtle and Miles stared at her, Kat said, "Her death solved a lot of problems for me, for sure." When they continued to stare at her, she gave a short laugh. "Hey, *I* didn't kill her. But I'm glad someone else did so that I didn't have to."

Tentatively, Myrtle said, "I've heard that Tammy left you and Dina a nice legacy, Kat."

Kat nodded her pink head. "I was really glad to hear about it. I want to upgrade the shop and bring in some more people. You know, maybe a younger clientele and another couple of girls to do hair."

"I was surprised that Tammy had such a substantial amount to pass on. Especially with her drinking problem."

"She probably drank a lot of it away, but she didn't spend money on other stuff. And she had a lot of it to go through. Her grandmother got filthy rich a few years ago from winning a malpractice lawsuit. Then she passed away the next year. My mom didn't get a cent because my grandmother wasn't even speaking to her by then. I wish Granny had sent some to *me*, but it was her money to do with what she wanted."

Kat said, "I'm going to use her money to turn over a new leaf, which is what *Tammy* should have used it for. The Beauty Box needs some sprucing up, too. I started just getting rid of the old magazines. Once I did that, the tables looked all stained and beat up, so I put in some nicer ones. The new tables made me realize how bad the walls looked, so I took down the tacky hair posters and started painting yesterday. It'll be a whole new Beauty Box by the time I'm done."

Kat glanced at her watch. "Hey, it was good talking, but I've got to run. I've got a two o'clock and Dina is holding down the fort while I'm gone...if *she* hasn't gone AWOL and headed for the shelter, that is."

Myrtle said, "She's still spending a lot of time over there?"

Kat nodded. "Every spare minute. Not that it's really a bad thing. But she's kind of going overboard with it. She must have been voted "Most Likely to Join a Cult" in her high school yearbook."

Miles watched Kat leave. "So what do you think, Sherlock? Did Kat do it?" he asked in a low voice.

Myrtle took a sip from her sweet tea before stage whispering, "I hope not. I really like her. But she *could* have murdered Tammy, sure."

Miles said, "She sure had the opportunity. She spent almost as much time at the Beauty Box as Dina. She could have easily come back there that night, killed Tammy, then returned to "discover" her the next morning."

Myrtle nodded, slowly. "She could have. But I don't know. It seems like you and I are missing something." She thought for a minute, sipping her tea. "Nope, can't pin it down." Myrtle pulled out her cell phone. "I forgot I had this thing on vibrate while we were at our stakeout."

"Did somebody call?"

Myrtle nodded, putting in her voice mail code. "It's Agnes. She says she has a tip for the column. I don't know why everybody is suddenly so flush with tips. I go for months with nothing and am begging people to send me something. Maybe Sloan is trying to beef up my column since he's so low on content for the paper right now. I guess I'll call her when I get back home."

"So, based on everything you know today," said Miles, "which suspect are you leaning toward?"

"Bootsie," said Myrtle firmly. "Or, well, maybe Kat or Dina. I know Tammy was babbling on about her will and changing it—if they knew they were getting money, that might have been reason for murder. Oh, who knows. This case has been a doozy."

IT WAS STILL DARK OUTSIDE when Myrtle woke up the next morning. Thinking a cool breeze or chirping crickets would help her sleep, she'd left her window open all night. Unfortunately, Myrtle had awakened sticky from the moist, heavy summer air. She showered and dressed in a cool cotton top and skirt.

This was the day she'd promised Prissy she'd read at Little Lambs Preschool. She cleared her throat of its early-morning gruffness and tried out a syrupy storytelling voice that she imagined Prissy might approve of. *No good.* She fell back on her technique from forty-five years ago: silly sound effects and vigorous gesticulating.

Myrtle was about to head out for an early-morning walk when she saw Jo ringing Elaine's doorbell. Wasn't it too early for her to be there? And...wasn't it the wrong day?

Jo was just bringing in her cleaning supplies and vacuum when Myrtle joined her. "Don't you come a different day, Jo?"

"You're right. But it's Agnes Walker's day and she's not answering her door. I hate to write her off my schedule completely, so if it's okay with you, I'll swap your days out and get to her on your day. Do you mind?" she asked Elaine.

Elaine looked over at the pile of dirty dishes in the kitchen sink and smiled. "Today works out great for me." She walked into the den with Jo while Myrtle slowly pulled out her cell phone and sat down at Elaine's kitchen table. She dialed Agnes' number and the phone rang eight, nine, ten times. Agnes had banned most modern devices—like answering machines—from her home, so there was no way to leave a message.

Myrtle tried Connor Walker's number. After a few rings, he picked up the phone and helloed in a rushed voice. "You're probably leaving for work," said Myrtle, "but I wondered if your mother was over there. Or if you'd heard from her lately."

Connor was pulling on his shoes, eating breakfast, and talking at the same time. No, his mother wasn't there and he hadn't talked to her recently. "I wouldn't worry about Mother, but it's nice for you to check up on her. She's getting a little deaf these days, so maybe she didn't hear the phone ring. Old age kicking in," he said a little apologetically. "By the way, thanks for introducing me to Kat. Funny thing how Tammy never managed to let us meet."

"I'm sure you two would have met each other eventually. Kat isn't exactly easily overlooked. I just helped speed up the process." She paused. "Are y'all officially going out then?"

"We've got a dinner date in a few nights. Looking forward to it."

The loud shuffling of papers and the briefcase snapping on Connor's end of the line reminded Myrtle that he was more interested in leaving than in finding his missing mother or discussing his social life, so Myrtle ended the conversation and hung up. She couldn't shake the nagging feeling that something was wrong. She grimaced at her watch. It was almost time for her to leave for the preschool. "Elaine," she called.

Elaine walked into the kitchen. "Just getting Jo started. What's wrong?" she asked quickly, seeing Myrtle's frown.

"Probably nothing," admitted Myrtle. "But it's a little strange that I couldn't reach Agnes yesterday afternoon or this morning, and she didn't answer the doorbell for Jo a few minutes ago. Let's check on her on the way to Little Lambs Preschool."

"Sure, that's no problem," said Elaine. She added in a low voice, "I don't mind leaving Jo here alone. After all, if Bootsie trusts her alone in her castle, I don't think I have anything to worry about."

After securing Jack in his car seat, they drove to Agnes' house. Myrtle stayed in the car with Jack and anxiously watched Elaine hurry up the carefully swept walkway and stairs to the wrap-around verandah. Elaine rang the doorbell, rapped loudly on the door, and peered through the sheer curtains in Agnes' windows. She tried the door and found it locked. Elaine shrugged at Myrtle and walked back to the car.

"Sorry, Myrtle. I guess she's not there."

Myrtle shook her head. "She wouldn't be out anywhere yet. The only early appointment she keeps is for the Beauty Box and this isn't her day. Besides, she was supposed to be here for Jo." She opened her car door. "I'm going to try the back door."

"Won't you be late to the school?"

"It'll only take a minute. I just want to be sure..." Myrtle pinched her mouth shut and walked quickly down the front walk, her cane punctuating the stones with thumps. As she walked around the side of the house, a sense of foreboding settled over her. "Agnes," she called as she approached the backyard.

Agnes' yardman came by each week to do the grunt work in her garden so that she could enjoy tending the flowers. She had a large rose garden currently in full bloom and rows of perennials on several sides of the yard. Myrtle noticed that the wrought-iron patio table held a tray with a couple of glasses and a pitcher.

Then she saw a crumpled body in a bright blue oxford shirt and worn khakis on the other side of the table. Myrtle, feeling as though she were floating, walked over to the body. Agnes lay on her face; the back of her head was smashed in. A dark-stained shovel lay next to her. Myrtle felt a tremendous sadness rush over her as she looked at her friend, who now seemed so small and frail and old on the ground.

It was obvious Agnes was dead. Myrtle leaned heavily on her cane as she walked across the patio to the back door. It was unlocked and Myrtle cautiously entered, careful not to touch anything. She took a tissue from her pocketbook and picked up the phone to call Red. When he answered, Myrtle said quietly, "Red. Get Lieutenant Perkins and come over to Agnes'. She's been murdered." Suddenly feeling very tired, Myrtle set the phone down on its receiver.

She glanced around the room. Agnes' house was as neat as ever, and Myrtle wondered why Agnes even needed Jo to clean for her. There was only a lone china cup in the spotless sink. As she walked through the living room toward the front door, she noticed suitcases on the floor near the door leading to the hallway—the only things that seemed to be out of place. There was no sign of any struggle in the house. Still using the tissue, she unlocked the front door and walked out.

Elaine grabbed her cell phone as soon as she saw Myrtle's face. "Need me to call Red?" she asked as she helped Myrtle into the minivan.

Myrtle shook her head and plopped onto the front seat. "No, I called him from inside the house."

"Is she—?" asked Elaine.

Myrtle's hard expression stayed set as she gave Elaine a curt nod.

Elaine and Myrtle sat silently during the few minutes it took for Red to arrive. Perkins' car and Red's drove up simultaneously. The men hurried to the minivan and Myrtle directed them to the back yard.

Soon there was a swarm of police at Agnes' house. Red left the crime scene to notify Connor of his mother's death. One policeman drove Myrtle to Red's office, which was in a small building that also housed the post office and town government. A sergeant with a watchful eye and a pitcher of ice water joined her. He called her "sweetheart" a couple of times, which usually would have fired Myrtle into a temper but passed completely unnoticed by her this time.

When Detective Lieutenant Perkins entered Red's office, the sergeant picked up a notebook and sat down in a chair in the corner of the room. Perkins thoughtfully eyed Myrtle as he poured a glass of water from the pitcher on Red's desk.

"You've had a tough morning," he said.

"I'm fine," she replied. When he tilted his head doubtfully and squinted at her with appraising eyes, she sat up straighter. "I'm fine," she repeated in a firm voice. Maybe she could convince herself that was the truth.

"How long have you known Agnes Walker? Did you know her well?"

Myrtle supposed he was easing her into the questioning to give her some time to regain her composure. "We'd known each other since we were children. We weren't playmates back then, of course...I'm a good bit older than she was." Myrtle shrugged.

Detective Lieutenant Perkins watched her with a steady gaze. "How would you describe her?"

"Well, she was very intelligent." Myrtle studied the ceiling. "No nonsense. Immaculately dressed and always smelling like talcum powder. She had a good sense of humor..." Myrtle shrugged again, not sure what Perkins was driving at.

"Can you think of anyone who would have wanted to kill her? Did she make many enemies?"

"Tammy didn't like her, but other than that I think Agnes was very well-liked."

"Why did Tammy dislike her?"

"Because Agnes didn't think Tammy was good enough to date her son. And because Tammy *knew* she wasn't good enough for Connor."

"And you can't think of anyone else who disliked her? Or another reason why she'd have been murdered?"

Myrtle remembered Agnes' mysterious warnings and the hunch that she was holding something back. Perkins sat patiently. Myrtle decided she wouldn't disclose that information for the time being. It was nothing concrete, after all...only a feeling on her part. She shook her head.

Detective Lieutenant Perkins said, "Going back to the murder scene now, Mrs. Clover. Why did you check up on Mrs. Walker this morning?"

"I kept feeling like something was wrong. Not that she'd been murdered, though. Maybe that she'd fallen down and couldn't reach the telephone. Plus, I hadn't been able to reach her on the phone, and her housekeeper said Agnes hadn't answered the door this morning when she went by to clean."

The sergeant looked up from his note-taking at the mention of the housekeeper and exchanged glances with Perkins. Myrtle rolled her eyes and said, "I'm sure Jo had nothing to do with it. Why on earth would she want to kill Agnes? It was the easiest gig in town: cleaning a spotless house."

"So from what I understand, the front door was locked when Elaine tried it. You entered the house from the back door after finding Mrs. Walker in the yard?"

"That's right. I called Red from inside the house. I unlocked the front door to leave. So I suppose the killer could have come through the bushes to avoid being seen."

Perkins asked, "Did anything in the house or grounds look unusual to you? Out of place or out of the ordinary?"

"Besides the elderly body in the back yard you mean?" asked Myrtle caustically. "No, everything in the house was as neat as usual. The suitcases were out of place, of course. Maybe she was planning to take a trip after all the stress of this investigation. And I thought it strange there would have been a pitcher of lemonade out and two glasses. Either she was expecting company or the murderer was her company, I suppose. Which means it was someone she knew."

Perkins leaned closer over Red's desk. "Does that surprise you, considering she didn't have any enemies?"

"Well, I didn't think it was some sort of thug roaming the countryside, no. Obviously, the murderer is someone we all know."

Perkins paused again, but when Myrtle offered nothing else on the subject, he said, "We're trying to track down the time the crime occurred. Could you tell me when you attempted to contact her?"

Myrtle rubbed her hands over her face. "Let's see. I'd just finished with lunch when I checked my messages. It must have been around quarter to three yesterday when I first tried to call her back."

"Did you try again later?"

Myrtle felt a wave of guilt. "Just once last night. I forgot to try her again after that. I tried to call again early this morning."

"When do you think she was most likely to have been in her gardening clothes and doing yard work?"

"I'm sure she got an early start, considering how hot it's been lately. She was probably in the yard at nine and then took a break to call me at ten."

"So you're assuming she was killed yesterday."

Myrtle frowned. "Yes. Because I couldn't reach her yesterday afternoon. Isn't that what the police think happened?"

"That's the preliminary consensus, yes." He paused again. "Was Mrs. Walker planning on leaving town for any reason? Do you know why she had her suitcases out?"

"I have no idea. I don't think she was planning on going anywhere at all." Exhaustion settled on her. "Is that all, Detective Lieutenant? I'd like to go home."

"That's all for now." In an unexpectedly gentle voice he added, "You've had a tough day, Mrs. Clover. Why don't you go home and rest?"

With her hand on the doorknob, Myrtle turned to Perkins and asked in alarm, "What time is it?"

"It's noon."

"Shoot!"

"Something wrong, Mrs. Clover?"

"I was supposed to be reading to Prissy's preschoolers an hour and a half ago," she groaned.

"You have a good excuse for your tardiness," the detective reminded her as Myrtle slowly moved out the door.

Elaine greeted her with concern. "I dropped Jack off at the sitter's house before I came over. Will you be okay?"

Myrtle said sadly, "I'll be all right. It's just such a waste. She was one of my few remaining friends, too." Elaine squeezed Myrtle's arm as she helped her into the minivan.

"Do you think we could run by the preschool before going home?"

Elaine smacked her forehead with a resounding slap that made Myrtle wince. "I completely forgot about Prissy. Sorry, I could have called her for you and let her know if I'd thought of it. Why don't I call and tell her what happened? You don't need to go by there when you're already so drained."

"I have a feeling that Prissy would expect more than a phone call. Standing up her little ones is probably a capital offense in her book."

When Myrtle and Elaine arrived at Little Lambs Preschool, the children were standing next to a carpool line, waiting for their moms. Prissy glared at Myrtle and Elaine while she opened sliding minivan doors and helped buckle kids into their car seats. Myrtle noticed again the strength in Prissy's arms as she easily plucked up the children and hoisted them into their seats. When the last student was whisked away, Prissy strode toward them.

Prissy was just opening her mouth when Myrtle said, "Before you say anything, I need to let you know some bad news. Agnes Walker was murdered this morning."

Prissy turned white. "Let's go into my office," Prissy said hoarsely. She led them down a short hall decorated with a brightly colored mural of nursery rhyme characters. Her office was a book-crammed cubby with a tall, leaded glass window and windowsill lined with African violets in green plastic pots. The children's construction paper art-work—all featuring trees, suns, and flowers—hung on the walls.

"What happened?" Prissy whispered anxiously. Her thin hands were now worrying the buttons on her twin-set sweater. Myrtle wondered how she could stand to wear a sweater in 90-degree weather.

Wearily, Myrtle again summarized the events of the morning. Prissy grew more agitated as she listened. "It must be some crazy person behind all this. Who would kill Agnes?"

"I don't think it's a maniac roaming the countryside," said Myrtle. "Someone amoral, sure, but not someone who's killing indiscriminately. There must be a reason behind it."

"Tammy made too many enemies to be murdered for no reason," Elaine reminded her gently. "And Agnes must have known something or seen something that made her dangerous to the murderer."

Since Prissy was so off-kilter, Myrtle decided to try pushing her over the brink. She pulled out one of Prissy's paperback books from her large pocketbook and held it up for Prissy's horrified gaze. "I picked this up from the Book Nook the other day. Not appropriate reading material for the kids, but I thought *you* might be interested, Prissy."

Myrtle continued sternly, "I'm sure your books were what Tammy was referring to that day in the Beauty Box when she rambled on about you not being as sweet as you seemed. For heaven's sake, Prissy, writing isn't a felony! Why are you being so coy about it?"

"You *were* sneaking around on my computer," Prissy hissed, looking at Myrtle with loathing. "How dare you!"

"I did. I'll admit it. I thought I'd find evidence of something really foul, like pornography or something, on there. I don't think you should have to be so secretive about this. Most people would be proud of being a published author."

Prissy stamped her foot. "Because I don't *want* people to know about it. Why else would I keep it a secret?" Elaine and Myrtle shared a mystified look as she continued ranting. "I have an upstanding position in this community. These moms *trust* me," she stressed. "I didn't want them to know about my writing and they didn't need to know about it!"

"Why would you write racy romances if you don't like them?" asked Myrtle.

Pure fury unleashed a different Prissy. "I needed more income and I wanted to stay at home to get it. Those books were easy for me to write."

Myrtle leveled her gaze at Prissy. "You *did* shove me that day at your house."

"I did not. But if I had, could you blame me? You had no business snooping around in my bedroom and opening documents on my computer. That was personal property." She clenched her thin fists. "You're not going to tell everyone about my books?" It sounded like a threat.

Myrtle shook her head. "No, Prissy, I won't say anything to anyone but the police. You seem very anxious that your secret stays safe. I have to ask you—did you kill Tammy to keep her from telling everyone?"

Prissy's face was sulky. "No. But I hated her and wasn't a bit sorry that someone killed her. I accidentally dropped a manuscript page at the salon one day when I was pulling out my checkbook. She stashed it away to read it later, then she tormented me about it until the day she died."

Elaine asked, "Did she try to blackmail you?"

Prissy answered, "No. Blackmail would have been a relief. She'd just drop big hints or make double-entendres. I don't think she needed money or cared about it. She just enjoyed making trouble." Prissy's long face was anxious at the memory. "I couldn't sleep at night, wondering when she'd get tired of it and finally tell the whole town about my books."

Exhaustion caught up with Myrtle again and she was suddenly eager to leave Little Lambs Preschool and put her feet up. "Prissy, how about if I come back next week to read? You'll make an excuse to the children for today?"

Prissy, competent preschool director, made a return appearance, "Of course. I made up an excuse today, as a matter of fact. I didn't want the children to think they'd been forgotten about when they were looking forward to the story." She hesitated. "I'm sorry about Mrs. Walker. She was...a great lady."

Elaine helped Myrtle into the car. As they drove away, they saw Prissy's thin figure watching them through the tall window of her office.

Chapter Fifteen

The next morning, Myrtle walked into the Beauty Box for her scheduled wash and set. Kat's non-smoking campaign wasn't going very well—she had a full ashtray next to her and was smoking what looked like the last cigarette in the pack. Kat slouched in a vinyl styling chair but stood up and stubbed out her cigarette when she saw Myrtle. "Sorry," Kat said. "Nerves."

Myrtle glanced around the deserted salon. "Where's everybody hiding, Kat? The Beauty Box is usually crammed with ladies by now."

"We got a couple of calls this morning to reschedule. Dina's at the shelter. And...today was Mrs. Walker's usual morning to come in, of course." Kat looked at Myrtle and raised the cigarette to her mouth again, before realizing that she'd stubbed it out. She gave a short laugh and tossed the butt into a wastebasket. "Everybody's freaked out. I'm not immune to it, either." She turned an inquisitive eye on Myrtle. "I didn't expect to see you here, after the day you had yesterday."

Myrtle nodded. "It was pretty awful. How did you hear about it? Were you at the Beauty Box yesterday morning?" There wasn't a good way to ask someone if they had an alibi.

Fortunately, Kat didn't seem to mind. "Actually, I saw Mrs. Walker when I was coming in. She was already out in her yard and I made some kind of comment about how early she was working. She said she was trying to beat the heat. Then I went inside. The next thing I saw was the police cars out front and you and Elaine sitting in her car." She shook her head and washed her hands to get ready to do Myrtle's hair.

"So you didn't see or hear anything else? Didn't notice anyone who shouldn't be there?"

"No. And I wish I had. I was busy getting the shop ready for the customers. I took towels out of the dryer, moved some of the paint cans and all...tried to get organized." She gave a short laugh.

"Was Dina around?" asked Myrtle. "Maybe she saw something. After all, Agnes lives right next door."

Kat made a face. "She *should* have been around, but she wasn't. I think she was over at the shelter again. I swear, she's driving me nuts with it. I'm glad she's found something that makes her happy, but if she doesn't start doing some work around here, I'm going to have to look for a new manicurist."

She seemed a little too agitated to be doing hair, so Myrtle carefully pointed the direction of the conversation back to the shop and how much better it was looking.

Kat's face lit up as she talked about paint swatches, curtains, new equipment and other things. In the place of the tatty magazines that used to be there, there were stacks of self-help paperbacks with titles like *Twelve Steps to Financial Freedom*. Kat seemed to be transforming, too. There were fewer earrings on fewer visible body parts. Myrtle moved over to the chair at the sink and listened as Kat expertly scrubbed her hair and chatted.

"Is your afternoon going to be this quiet, too?" asked Myrtle.

"Let's hope not. I'd go broke if that were the case. No, I've got Bootsie Davenport coming in for her new do."

"I like the way you're doing it now. Is she just coming in to get it styled?"

"She's thinking about adding a little color to it. She's wanted to update her look for a long time but Tammy was in no shape to do it. Plus, Tammy would have been furious if she'd tried to switch over to me."

She sure would have been. It would have been Bootsie's death they'd have been investigating, instead of Tammy's. "So, is there anything else you're planning to do with the Beauty Box?"

"I'm thinking about installing some tanning beds in Tammy's old room. I think that might bring in some people. There really aren't any tanning beds anywhere near to Bradley."

"How about...paintings?" asked Myrtle.

Kat frowned. "Paintings?"

"Mmm-hmm. I've got a lovely painting of Miles and me surrounded by books. I'd be happy to donate it to a worthy cause like the rebirth of the Beauty Box."

"Oh. I really *appreciate* it, Miss Myrtle, but I don't think a book painting will fit in with the new décor. It's really nice of you, though."

Shoot.

AFTER MAKING HER WAY back home, Myrtle fixed a pimento cheese sandwich for lunch. She'd just finished when the phone rang. It was a solemn Connor Walker calling, wanting to hear about yesterday morning. She recounted the day, avoiding her usual melodramatic retelling, and asked if there was anything she could do to help him out.

"Actually, I did want to ask you a favor. Could you go in her closet and pick out an outfit for Mother to be buried in? I don't have a clue what she'd have wanted. And I know she would have wanted things perfect."

"Your mother certainly would have. Which reminds me, you might like Jo to clean your mother's house a little before your visitation there tomorrow. Your mom kept a perfect house, but she *was* due for her regular cleaning. Want me to let Jo in to vacuum and dust?"

"That would be great. Mother would have wanted it spruced up with half the town going over there."

"I'll run by your house in a little while for the key."

She was hanging up when the doorbell rang, making her jump. Exercising more caution than usual, Myrtle peered out the dining room curtains. When she saw Red, she opened the door.

"Hi, Red." He looked distracted. Was that a good condition for him to be in for her to get information? She couldn't remember. "Uh...would you like some lunch? I've got a casserole I defrosted last night. It's pretty good."

Red shuddered. "Uh, no, that's okay. I'll grab some lunch after I meet with Perkins."

He plopped down at her kitchen table and fidgeted with the tablecloth. Myrtle said, "Okay Red. Spit it out. To what do I owe the honor of this visit?"

Red took a deep breath. "The letter you received. The warning? It was clipped from a newspaper we found in Agnes' desk."

"Agnes? Why on earth would she have done that?"

Red shrugged. "I don't know, Mama. Maybe she was just concerned with your well-being?"

"No," scoffed Myrtle. "She'd have warned me in person, like she'd already done." She frowned. "Agnes was trying to scare me off the case."

"Although that sure wasn't possible," mumbled Red.

"That means she must have pegged Connor as the killer," mused Myrtle. "She must've seen something and been trying to cover up for him."

"That could well be," said Red. "But we haven't been able to get anything on him so far. Maybe she thought you were on the verge of finding out something we weren't." He paused for a moment. "I don't suppose Agnes could have done it. She was elderly, but one heck of a strong woman."

"I guess she *could* have done it, but I don't think she did. Besides, who killed Agnes if she killed Tammy?"

"Someone avenging Tammy's death?"

"Who? And why? No one even liked Tammy anymore."

Red wearily rubbed his eyes. "I don't know, Mama. All I know is that letter came from Agnes Walker's house." He peeked out hopefully behind his hands. "Does this murder make you think twice about trying to figure out who's behind this?"

"Not a chance!"

Red glowered at her. "I think you'd be a lot safer off at Greener Pastures Retirement Home, Mama."

"I think I have a darling gnome collection that needs to be aired out in my front yard."

"I think I actually might schedule an admissions interview for you," said Red.

"I think I might commission Elaine to do a portrait of you. It can hang in a place of honor in your house."

Red exhaled with a hiss and quickly took his leave.

THERE WERE ALREADY at least a dozen casseroles (half of them Chicken Divan) in freezer-appropriate, labeled, and dated containers by the time Myrtle made it over to Connor's house. There were even some hand-written notes of condolence on the front table.

In the case of a single man like Connor, it would be assumed by the well-meaning ladies of the church that he wouldn't be aware of anything that needed to be done for the funeral. Mrs. Dawkins, a gray-haired dragon, was dispatched from Agnes' church circle to drop in on Connor. She arrived bearing a steno pad and pencil and demanding information for the obituary. The annoying thing about Mrs. Dawkins was that she kept asking questions that she clearly knew the answers to. "Your mother held office for the Bradley Garden Club, didn't she?" Connor would look a little confused, and Mrs. Dawkins would jot down, "President, Bradley Garden Club, 1996."

"I'd advise," said Mrs. Dawkins with a sniff, "that Agnes' obituary also run in the *Charlotte Observer*. And I'd strongly urge that it run in the Roanoke, Virginia, paper too."

"Why on earth should it run there?" asked Myrtle.

"Roanoke was Agnes' birthplace." Mrs. Dawkins looked displeased by the insurrection.

"Seventy-five years ago," said Myrtle, "and Agnes' parents moved to Bradley when she was a baby. Which I *remember*." She wasn't above pulling the age card.

"Well, I think it's proper."

"I think it's silly," said Myrtle. "Besides, all the people who remember when Agnes was born are all probably dead."

Mrs. Dawkins ignored Myrtle and continued stiffly making plans for the service. She grunted in disapproval when she learned the service would be several days away—quick burials being the norm in the South. She apparently found Connor's mention of the autopsy the final straw and left quickly afterward.

"What a relief," said Myrtle. "Hope the door hit her on the way out."

Connor seemed to be hiding a smile. "I guess funeral preparations are complicated. Mrs. Dawkins was trying to help."

"They don't seem complicated to me. And believe me, I'm old enough to have gone to a ton of them." Connor did look fairly stressed out, however. "How are *you* doing?"

His face darkened. "I'm furious. Tammy is one thing, because she pushed people's buttons, but who could have killed my mother? For what reason?"

"It's crazy, isn't it? Do you think she knew something, or thought she knew something?" asked Myrtle.

Connor was quiet, then answered, "I did go back to the Beauty Box the night of Tammy's murder. I wanted to tell Tammy I was sorry for everything I'd said and sorry that things hadn't worked out for us. I was hoping to stay on speaking terms with her, even if we weren't ever going to be friends again." He gave a short laugh. "This town is too small for me to be on fighting terms with anybody."

Agnes Walker's dining room window was in plain view of the front of the Beauty Box. "So your mother saw your car pull up to the Beauty Box, I'm guessing. What time was that, Connor?"

He was thoughtful. "I'd gone home after the fight with Tammy, let off some steam. It must have been about ten-forty-five. I pulled up to the shop and parked in front. Then I walked around back to knock on Tammy's bedroom door. I knocked on her door and called her name. The lights were off, so I figured she'd gone somewhere. She usually turns on every light in the house when she's there."

"Was Dina there?" asked Myrtle.

"Not that I noticed."

"How long were you there?"

"I figured Dina and Tammy might have gone out together for a walk or something. They used to do that before Tammy started drinking so much. I felt like I'd been put through the wringer, so I pulled out my cigarettes and had one. I just sat there on the step. I must have been there twenty-five minutes or more. Then I gave up and walked back to the front of the shop and drove off."

Myrtle said, "So your mother saw your car leave. And she thought you'd be considered a suspect."

Connor nodded. "Which I would have been. Tammy and I had argued out in public, and I came over to see her afterwards. I told Mother that I had nothing to be worried about—I hadn't done it and there was no proof that I had." His face was somber. "Mother was in a state. I thought she might have a stroke or a heart attack or something. She didn't want even the faintest hint of a scandal. She made me swear that I wouldn't say anything about being over there. I wasn't exactly eager to put myself at the scene of the crime, but my first thought was actually for Mother. I promised her I wouldn't say a word. After all, I knew

I *hadn't* killed Tammy. She convinced me it might distract the police from finding the actual murderer."

Agnes probably worried, deep down, that Connor had killed Tammy. Twenty-five minutes was plenty of time to have stabbed Tammy and pushed her down the stairs, and obviously Agnes hadn't seen anyone else coming or going at the Beauty Box. But Agnes wouldn't have spent the whole evening at her dining room window; there would have been plenty of opportunities for the murderer to slip in or out.

Connor sighed. "I wish I'd told the police. Mother was behaving in a very cloak-and-dagger way. She must've given the murderer the impression she knew more than she did."

The doorbell rang. Kat stood holding a casserole at Connor's front door. Connor's face lit up when he saw her and Myrtle doubted it was because Kat was carrying yet another dish of Chicken Divan.

"You look great, Kat," noted Myrtle, studying the girl's toned-down hair. It was now a more natural black color with pink highlights. Myrtle guessed that black must be close to Kat's actual hair color.

"Thanks, Miss Myrtle. Since I'm a salon owner now, I wanted a more professional look. But I couldn't give up the pink altogether. I worked on it this afternoon."

Connor said, "Uh-oh. Slow again over there?"

"Yes, but things are picking up again. I was going to dye it earlier, but then everything went nuts. Dina was going to dye it for me the night Tammy died, but she chickened out after I was sitting in the chair and had gotten the dye mixed and all the equipment out. Probably just as well, considering what Dina did to your poor mom's hair."

Myrtle asked, "Dina didn't want to dye it?"

"No, I apparently intimidated her a little. Her hands were shaking so much when she was pulling the gloves on and getting the colors set up that I was glad when she backed out right before squirting the dye on me."

Connor snorted. "Yeah, you might have ended up with bright blue hair like my mom. Thank God you dyed it back for Mother. She was furious with Dina."

Figuring that Kat would cheer him up more than she would, Myrtle said, "I'd better go. Let me know if you need anything else, Connor. And thanks for the key to your mother's."

Myrtle walked briskly to Agnes' bedroom to find her burial outfit. The house seemed like a mere shell without Agnes there providing some soul for the place. She frowned again at the out of place suitcases which was the only sign of untidiness in the house. Really, it just needed some dusting and a vacuum. Myrtle pulled a well-tailored and long-skirted navy suit out of the closet and draped them on the bed for Connor to take to the funeral home later, let Jo and her cleaning supplies in, and left for home. There was really only one remedy for a day such as today. A mind-numbing viewing of a poorly-written soap opera.

Tomorrow's Promise was already in progress by the time she settled down in front of it. And, as usual, the characters were making horrible mistakes. Sally once again took her cheating louse of an ex-husband back. Timothy was bound and determined to join that cult that anyone could see was full of loonies. Denise was having another affair with a man young enough to be her son—possibly even her grandson, considering how well-preserved she was. And Tony was packing his suitcases to leave Trisha and their baby.

It was the suitcases that made Myrtle stop and think. And then stop and think some more.

Chapter Sixteen

"**M**iles, we need to set a trap."

Miles' voice sounded rather sleepy. "Have you collected more feral cats, Myrtle? Isn't one ferocious feline enough for you?"

"No, no, I mean a trap for the *murderer*. I don't want to plot this over the phone—can't you come by? You're not sleeping, are you?"

Now Miles' voice had an edge of irritation to it. "Actually, I was putting my feet up for a little while, yes. I didn't sleep so well last night."

"Miles, I haven't slept for the past five years and I'm doing all right. Plus I'm a good ten or fifteen years older than you. Can't you just come over?"

Challenges were clearly key to get Miles motivated. He was walking through Myrtle's front door mere minutes later. He wasn't in a good humor, but he was there. "You mentioned a trap?" he asked stiffly.

Myrtle was busily pouring Miles a small glass of red wine. "Here."

Miles frowned at the glass as he slowly took it from Myrtle. "Wine? At three-thirty in the afternoon?"

"Well, it's five o'clock somewhere, Miles. Since we're conspiring, I figured a little alcohol would fit in well. It should probably be liquor and we should be smoking cigars, but a little red wine will fit."

Miles blinked at her. Sometimes he really did seem sort of slow. How on earth did he survive all those years as a pharmacist or whatever it was he did?

"So," said Myrtle, settling into her sofa with her own glass of wine, "The problem is that there's no *evidence* against Dina. So I think the only good solution is to have Dina try to *attack* me. Then you can catch her in the act, we can get Red over, and everything will unravel for her."

Miles' jaw dropped open, then closed and opened a few more times as if it were on a broken hinge. "*Dina*? What are you talking about, Myrtle? Dina hasn't killed anybody."

"On the contrary, she's killed two people. And I'm of the opinion that she's especially dangerous. No, we need to make sure that she's taken totally out of commission."

Miles still gaped. "What makes you think that Dina killed Tammy and Agnes?"

Myrtle smiled. It made her feel complacent to know something that no one else knew. "There were a couple of different things, really. But the main thing was those darned suitcases. The ones in the middle of Agnes' hall."

Miles nodded, but his eyes were completely blank.

Myrtle sighed. "You're not following? Well, Agnes was done traveling. She was completely adamant about it, actually. Her traveling days were over and done with. Why on earth would she have suitcases out? And empty ones, in the middle of her hall? For a minute I foolishly thought that maybe she was about to make a run for it—that *Agnes* was Tammy's killer. But then I thought about little Miss Dina. She'd come by gathering donations for the women's shelter—her new, favorite project. I think suitcases would make an eminently suitable donation for a women's shelter. Something sturdy for the women to put their things in while they're in transition. I'm sure Agnes would have felt the same way."

"I hate to point this out, Myrtle, but that doesn't mean that Dina *killed* Agnes. Why would she have done it, to begin with? And even if Agnes did set the suitcases out for Dina, it just means that Dina hadn't made it by to collect them before Agnes died."

"There's also the fact that Madam Zora saw suitcases in her crystal ball."

Miles stared at her, unblinkingly.

"Oh ye of little faith!" Really, Miles should be more trusting of her instincts by now. "Agnes clearly *saw* something. Now, she's been really focused on whether Connor was somehow involved, but obviously there must have been something else that she saw that suddenly made her think. I believe that Dina came over that morning to get the suitcases before clients started coming by the Beauty Box. Agnes must have asked her a very pointed question, and Dina freaked out and killed Agnes right there in her own backyard. She'd have forgotten about the donation by then."

Myrtle continued, "And it's not just the suitcases. Remember I told you that Red said the killer had worn gloves, even though it seemed like a heat-of-the-moment crime? It always struck me as sort of an anomaly. If it was a spontaneous crime of passion, why would the killer be wearing gloves? Then Kat told me that Dina was supposed to have dyed Kat's hair the night Tammy was murdered—as a practice run. Dina was all ready to start dyeing and then was too flustered to go through with it. We know how forgetful Dina is—Red mentioned that he saw her walking down the street holding hair shears and she nearly walked out with Jack's Dirty Doggy before I stopped her. When I was sitting with the Davenports at the diner, Dina came in with pink curlers in her hair. What if she still had the gloves on when Tammy returned from her meal with Connor? It all fits perfectly."

"Maybe it *fits*, but where's the *why* in all of this? Dina loved Tammy. For all intents and purposes, she's seemed totally devastated by her death." Miles took a restorative swig from his wine glass.

"Here's what I think happened. And I'll tell you what made me think of it...my soap opera. There's this character on *Tomorrow's Promise* who continues to get involved with these completely inappropriate men. They're these sort of brooding, ominous types. But finally, as sometimes happens in real life, the character snapped. She was put down one time too many, and she ended up killing the man she was involved with."

"And this reminds you of Dina and Tammy how?" asked Miles.

"We know Tammy's behavior was getting worse. What if Tammy upset Dina by dissing her? Dina had a lot of respect and appreciation for Tammy. But Tammy seemed totally scornful of Dina most of the time. What if Dina were afraid of being on her own again, and she lashed out at Tammy?"

Miles took his glasses off and rubbed them with a pressed handkerchief from his pants pocket. This usually meant he was about to suggest something that Myrtle wouldn't like. "If it all fits so perfectly, why don't we call up Red and Lieutenant Perkins and let them know? That way they can check it out and maybe even pressure a confession out of Dina."

Myrtle gave a scornful snort. "Do you really think Red is going to do anything about it?"

"Of course I do! It's his duty to check out that kind of thing, Myrtle. Didn't he take some sort of oath or something?"

"So what am I going to say to him? 'By the way, Red, Dina the manicurist is the killer. She gave away her identity with suitcases, latex gloves, a crystal ball clue, and a soap opera.'"

"Okay. Well, let me in on your plan. I can't wait to hear this one."

Myrtle leaned forward a little on the sofa. "Here's what I'm thinking. I'll lure Dina over to the house by letting her think that I know something. Which I do. You'll be skulking around and will take pictures or video when she starts coming after me."

"After which," interjected Miles in a dry voice, "she'll come after *both* of us. Since she's obviously not really in her right mind."

"So you'll be armed."

"With what?" Miles said cautiously. "I don't carry guns."

"Just a knife or a baseball bat or a hammer—something to smack her with."

Miles drained his wine and reached for the bottle to get a refill. "I don't like this idea, Myrtle. I'm filming Dina trying to kill you? I'm hitting a woman?"

"A *murderer*. You're hitting a *murderer*."

"Still."

"Here's the plan. Sloan Jones, over at the paper, has been sending me reminder emails about my investigative news story. He apparently desperately needs more content for the next issue. So I thought I'd do a recap story of what I've learned so far. But at the end, I'll explain that I'm hot on the trail of the killer and have found out something very interesting following the death of my friend, Agnes." Myrtle was dismayed at the lump in her throat. She cleared it with a cough. "Maybe I'll write a sort of tribute to Agnes, too. If it seems insensitive that I'm using Agnes' death to catch a murderer, just remember that Agnes would want her behind bars, too."

Miles nodded. "All right. So you're thinking that Dina will read the story and come after you? What if she doesn't read the paper?"

"Dina reads it every day, as far as I can tell. Seems to like the horoscope section with all the goofy made-up stuff. But read it she does. And I have a feeling she's following the crime stories pretty closely now."

"Okay. Well, tomorrow is off. I've got to go out of town and find a wedding gift for my niece. And I wanted to find some nice new towels for my out-of-town guests to use."

"There are stores here, Miles."

"But I need to get something *nice*. Which is harder to find here."

"All right. I'll go ahead and take the story over to Sloan and ask him to run it day-after-tomorrow. The papers are usually delivered around seven, so you can come here for breakfast and then hang out while I wait to get attacked."

"Sounds like a lovely day," said Miles grimly.

Myrtle sat in the cluttered newsroom of *The Bradley Bugle* and tapped her fingers on the small amount of desk that wasn't covered up with paper. She had her story ready to go. It was a masterpiece, really, considering what she was trying to do with it. It recapped what they knew so far, reported on Agnes' death (including a touching memorial in a separate story...that had actually made Myrtle tear up a bit), and then concluded with Myrtle's declaration that she knew exactly who the killer was and was only looking for evidence to support her discovery. Brilliant.

The wall clock showed four o'clock. Sloan should definitely still be in the office. She had other things to do, though. She put a sticky note on the top of the story with clear instructions not to run the story for another day. With any luck, Red and Elaine would be too busy to read the paper until Dina had had a chance to attack Myrtle.

Unfortunately, the sticky note wasn't very sticky at all. Soon it had curled up enough to fall off the paper and into the piles on the desk. When Sloan finally drove up to the *Bradley Bugle* building in his 1970s model Chevy and lugged his large frame into the newsroom, he never saw the little yellow sticky note. But he was delighted to see Myrtle's story since one of his regular columnists had fallen through and he needed about half a page of content for tomorrow's paper.

The next morning, Myrtle threw the paper onto her kitchen table without bothering to look at it. It was truly disturbing how the *Bradley Bugle* became more and more tabloid-y every day. The thing was full of celebrity news, local rumors, and silly opinions.

Myrtle plopped her last two eggs with some butter in the skillet to scramble, then happened to look out the window and notice that Erma had left her wheelbarrow right side up on *Myrtle's* side of the property line. It had rained last night, too, which meant there would be pesky mosquitoes breeding in the water. Mosquitoes that would likely only attack Myrtle since Erma apparently was immune. Probably had an understanding with the little beasts.

Myrtle grabbed her cane and stepped outside to tip the wheelbarrow over. She was turning to hurry back in when a shadow fell over her. "Dina," Myrtle said. For heaven's sake. She wasn't supposed to be here yet!

Dina said in a clear voice, "When you didn't answer your doorbell, I came around back. I let myself in through the back gate," she explained unnecessarily.

As Myrtle continued staring at her, Dina said, "Thought I'd drop by and see if you had any donations for the shelter." The sun glinted on the large lenses of her glasses, making it hard to see her eyes.

Myrtle answered, "No, I sure don't. Remember? Red helped me drop them off –you already collected things from me for the shelter."

Dina shifted from foot to foot. "Did I?"

"Was there another reason you're here, Dina?" She hoped it wasn't the one she thought it might be. With all the snooping that rotten neighbor Erma Sherman did, why couldn't she be gaping out her windows when she *needed* her to?

"I saw this article today. In the *Bugle*."

Shoot! That Sloan!

In a strange tone, Dina asked, "Do you? Do you know who the murderer is?"

Myrtle answered, "You are. You killed both Tammy and Agnes Walker."

"Why would I have killed Tammy?" asked Dina, almost as if she wanted it explained herself.

"I think," said Myrtle slowly, "that you must have just been tired of being put down. That's only natural, isn't it? I was watching my soap opera—you watch *Tomorrow's Promise*, don't you?"

Dina nodded.

"Remember how Sally kept going for the wrong men? And they always pushed her around and were hateful to her?" asked Myrtle.

Dina said, "Then one day Sally snapped. And she killed Stone, who was the last man who was ugly to her."

"Exactly!" said Myrtle, beaming at Dina. "It wasn't that Stone was any worse than the others, but he was the final straw. I think Tammy must have been your final straw. She was your friend, but she changed and started being verbally abusive to you. It must have reminded you of your ex-husband—in all the wrong ways."

"She got you set up at her shop and allowed you to be her roommate at the duplex in the other half of the Beauty Box. She knew how to push everyone's buttons. Maybe she told you how worthless you were. Useless to everyone. You couldn't understand how someone who had been so good to you could change so radically."

Dina said impassively, "I hated the way she was talking to me. But it wasn't just that. She said she was going to marry Connor Walker and wouldn't need me for a roommate anymore. After she got married, she planned on selling the Beauty Box. I'd be scrambling for a job and a place to stay again. By myself."

"You were supposed to be dyeing Kat's hair. But Tammy had really done a number on your self-esteem before she left with Connor. You weren't confident enough to dye Kat's hair. When Tammy came back home early, she'd been drinking and was in a very foul mood from being dumped by Connor. She needed someone to take it out on."

Dina looked mesmerized by Myrtle's story. Myrtle continued, "Tammy's murder had all the hallmarks of a crime of passion—spontaneous and unplanned. But the scissors were brand new and didn't have any fingerprints on them. The police believed that the killer wore gloves and the crime was premeditated."

Dina waited for Myrtle to give the explanation.

"But you've always been preoccupied and lately were even more absentminded than usual, since you had a lot on your mind. When you decided not to dye Kat's hair, you still wore the latex gloves when Tammy returned a few minutes later from her date with Connor."

Dina nodded again and Myrtle took a deep breath. "Tammy started in on you. She was scornful and bullying. You say that she threatened to turn you out of your home and close the shop where you worked. You were scared and upset and while her back was turned, you reached over and grabbed a pair of scissors and plunged them into Tammy's back. The door to the basement was open; Tammy had a basket of towels she was about to take downstairs and throw in the washer. You pushed her down the stairs."

Dina shivered. "There was blood everywhere."

"You appeared to have gotten away with it," Myrtle said quietly. "Then you discovered Tammy had left you money in her will."

Dina said, "She was helping me again, like she had at the beginning before she started drinking again. It reminded me of the old Tammy, the way she used to be. And it really made me mourn her more. She wasn't always a bad person."

"You wanted to do something good with the money, didn't you, to make up for what you'd done? You decided on a shelter for women like you who'd gone through the kinds of things that you had."

Dina's face changed when the subject of the shelter came up. Her face lit with fierce pride.

Myrtle went on, "For the first time in your life, you were independent, doing something you enjoyed and believed in. You were determined not to be found out. And you thought someone knew about it."

Dina said in a vacant voice, "Agnes Walker."

Myrtle leaned heavily on her cane for support on the damp ground. "She must have told you something that day you dyed her hair bright blue. She asked you awkward questions about when you were at the Beauty Box the night of Tammy's murder and what you'd seen. You thought she was asking them because she knew you'd done it. But she was actually asking them because she was trying to find out if you'd seen anything to implicate her son, Connor."

"Connor? She never mentioned that she thought that I knew something about *Connor*. She acted like she knew something," Dina's voice rose to a shrill. "Other clients came in and interrupted us. I thought she knew! I thought she'd seen me leave the Beauty Box that night to get rid of the gloves. Stupid, stupid of her not to tell me she thought it was Connor!"

"So you went to see Agnes and confront her. You probably made an excuse to drop by and pick up some shelter donations. You must have sneaked around the back when you heard her getting some early yard work done in the backyard."

Dina was quiet, so Myrtle continued. "Southern lady that she was, she went in the house and came out with lemonade and glasses. You started asking her questions about what she knew about the murder. Agnes must have gotten agitated, thinking you were angling that you knew something about Connor's part in the murder."

"I wasn't sure what she saw. I thought maybe she knew something." She held out her palms to Myrtle, "I couldn't go to jail for killing Tammy. The shelter is still just getting set up. Things were finally going really great for me. I couldn't let my life get messed up again right when everything was so wonderful."

Myrtle fixed Dina with a stern stare "You thought Agnes knew you'd killed Tammy. Thought Agnes was going to tell the police. You slipped on her gardening gloves, picked up the shovel her yardman left out the day before, and hit her with it as hard as you could."

"I had to stop her from telling everyone what she knew." Dina's lower lip quivered.

Myrtle said tiredly, "She didn't even know anything."

"But *you* knew," said Dina quietly. She edged closer to Myrtle. "You even told the paper that you knew!"

"And now it's time let the police know. Let's go inside and call Red now. It's over."

Dina's eyes held a wild expression. "No, Miss Myrtle. It can't be over. Not with everything finally going my way. Not with the shelter. They *need* me there." She took a couple of steps toward Myrtle with a deadly focus in her eyes and hands outstretched.

Chapter Seventeen

A sudden, piercing, wailing alarm blared behind them from the house. Dina swung around to look and Myrtle took the opportunity to raise her cane as far over her head as she could reach and bring it crashing down on Dina.

Dina *looked* like she was unconscious, but Myrtle had watched too many horror movies to just assume she wasn't going to rise up again and come after her. On the other hand, there actually was real smoke coming out of her kitchen window from the eggs she'd left on the stove. Red had installed those smoke detectors that he'd been so very fixated on. Bless him.

She had never been more relieved to see Miles' bespectacled face. He came rushing through her back gate clutching Elaine's abominable painting and looking back and forth from the figure on the ground to the smoke coming out of the kitchen.

"Call Red and make sure Dina doesn't get up off the ground, Miles. I'm going to put this fire out if it isn't too far gone already!" She turned toward the house, paused for a split second, turned quickly back to Miles, then rushed off again as fast as her old legs, hips, and knees could carry her.

Luckily, the smoke alarm that Red had surreptitiously installed in Myrtle's kitchen was extremely sensitive. And loud. She'd put out the fire with the handy kitchen fire extinguisher he'd so thoughtfully provided for her.

The other exciting moment came when a sergeant with the state police hauled a handcuffed Dina out of Myrtle's backyard. Detective Lieutenant Perkins joined her on the sofa. He opened his mouth, then closed it again and shook his head. "I'm not sure what to say, Mrs. Clover. On the one hand, you helped us apprehend the murderer, but on the other you interfered in police business and very nearly got yourself killed."

Myrtle ignored the last part. "Is this where I explain all my deductions and show you how clever I've been?"

Red walked into the room. He had obviously regained his composure. "Clever nothing, Mama. You meddled in our investigation and stumbled into discovering the murderer's identity. Shoot, you almost became a victim yourself. That would have just added a lot more work for us at the station. I can't believe you put that story in the paper to lure Dina."

Miles cleared his throat, "Actually, Red, Myrtle hadn't planned for the story to run today. It was going to run tomorrow, and I was going to tape Dina trying to attack your mother."

Red stared at Miles as if he'd lost complete use of his mind.

Myrtle drew herself up on the sofa. "Besides, I most certainly didn't *stumble* into anything. I put two and two together. I made deductions."

"And how exactly," asked Perkins, smoothly interrupting Red, who was starting to fuss again, "did you make these deductions?"

Myrtle beamed. "Well, the motive really came to me when I was watching *Tomorrow's Promise*." Perkins suppressed a groan. Red didn't bother suppressing his.

After Myrtle finished retelling her story, Red and Perkins looked thoughtfully at each other.

"I'm guessing that Dina used Agnes Walker's gardening gloves to keep from leaving prints on the shovel. We'll take a look through Dina's things and see if we can find the gloves there," said Perkins. "Although it's fairly incidental, considering that she confessed to us while we were still giving her the Miranda Rights."

Red's expression was baffled. "I never would have pegged Dina Peters for a killer. She's always been a little odd, but such an anxious, timid thing. And now her independence is gone for good. She sure went about *that* the wrong way." Myrtle was unable to get rid of the smug smile stretching across her face. "Your deductions may have been right on the nose, Mama, but you've done some pretty stupid stuff. Being nosy, questioning suspects in a murder investigation. Putting a story in the *Bradley Bugle*. I hope you realize how close you came to meeting your Maker."

Myrtle said calmly, "I think Dina ought to realize how close *she* came to meeting *hers*. After all, she's the one who ended up unconscious on the ground."

"But it was my smoke detector that created enough of a distraction for you to be able to crack her over the head with your cane."

"But it was *my scrambled eggs* that caused the smoke detector to go off to begin with."

Red rolled his eyes. "Like that was part of a master plan! For you, burning something is just called 'mealtime.' It's an everyday occurrence."

Myrtle gave him a stony look. "You know," she said, "I haven't put my gnomes out for a while. They get kind of cramped in that shed, you know. I think it might be time for a good airing out."

"All I'm doing, Mama, is questioning your judgment. And I think that's a reasonable thing to be assessing right now. It seems to me like you're making a lot of errors in judgment."

"And it seems to me like my gnomes need to revisit my front yard." Myrtle stood up from the sofa.

Perkins and Miles both started speaking at once, probably worried that the gnomes' appearance was going to coincide with their current visit and that they may somehow become enlisted. This sudden surge of conversation was interrupted as the front door burst open, and Elaine rushed in with Jack in tow.

"Myrtle!" she said, running over to give her a tight hug. "I can't believe it! *Dina*? I never would have picked Dina for a killer. And you brought her down on your own?"

"And nearly brought the house down with her," said Red morosely. At Elaine's confused look, Red said, "Mama set her house on fire by leaving a skillet of eggs on the stove."

Elaine covered her mouth with her hands. "Did you have a lot of damage?"

Myrtle sat back down on the sofa and folded her hands together. "I was able to put the fire out before it destroyed anything. Anything, *except*—," Myrtle spread her hands out wordlessly, looking sadly at Elaine. "Oh, Elaine. Tragically, your painting was destroyed by the spray of the extinguisher foam." Unfortunately, it really hadn't been because the kitchen extinguisher was full of a dry material like baking soda. Myrtle had had to run it under the kitchen sink a bit for good measure.

"It was—in the kitchen?" Elaine looked a little startled by this revelation. Miles made an oddly strangled sound, which he quickly covered up by emphatically blowing his nose in a handkerchief.

"Only so I could enjoy it while I cooked," explained Myrtle smoothly. "After all, cooking is such a chore for me that I need something to distract me."

Elaine sat down next to Myrtle and gave her another hug. "Don't worry a bit about it. The important thing is that you're okay! A murderous manicurist didn't kill you in your yard, and your house didn't burn down."

Red's face was the picture of careful concern. "Still, sweetie, maybe you could paint another picture for Mama. I know she and Miles enjoyed it so much." He gave his mother a sweet smile.

Myrtle gritted her teeth into a grin.

Elaine paused a second, then said, "I hate to say it, but I don't think I want to. I'm considering taking a cooking class, instead. Painting is all right, but it's not really as fun as I thought it was going to be. I think I'm done with the art world for a while."

Myrtle smiled understandingly.

Once Elaine and Jack left for home, Red looked at her admiringly. "All right, Mama. I'm sorry I questioned your judgment. You're obviously in full possession of your faculties if you were able to rid this world of that painting. Somehow managing to destroy it in the middle of all that chaos shows great presence of mind."

Myrtle raised an eyebrow. "So you're not impressed by my deductions, firefighting, or cane-wielding skills, but destroying art wins your approval?"

"If you want to put it that way." They sat thoughtfully for a moment.

Myrtle jumped a little as the doorbell rang. It was Puddin, who had clearly come over purely because of the police cars parked outside. "I just thought you might need some cleaning," she said with gleaming, green eyes.

"Actually, Puddin, you had *perfect* timing today," said Myrtle as she led the way into the kitchen. She heard Red chuckling behind her.

About the Author:

Elizabeth writes the Southern Quilting mysteries and Memphis Barbeque mysteries for Penguin Random House and the Myrtle Clover series for Midnight Ink and independently. She blogs at ElizabethSpannCraig.com/blog, named by Writer's Digest as one of the 101 Best Websites for Writers. Elizabeth makes her home in Matthews, North Carolina, with her husband. She's the mother of two.

Sign up for Elizabeth's free newsletter to stay updated on releases: https://elizabethspanncraig.com/newsletter/

This and That

I love hearing from my readers. You can find me on Facebook as Elizabeth Spann Craig Author, on Twitter as elizabethscraig, on my website at elizabethspanncraig.com, and by email at elizabethspanncraig@gmail.com.

Thanks so much for reading my book...I appreciate it. If you enjoyed the story, would you please leave a short review on the site where you purchased it? Just a few words would be great. Not only do I feel encouraged reading them, but they also help other readers discover my books. Thank you!

Did you know my books are available in print and ebook formats? And most of the Myrtle Clover series is available in audio. Find them on Audible or iTunes.

Interested in having a character named after you? In a preview of my books before they're released? Or even just your name listed in the acknowledgments of a future book? Visit my Patreon page at https://www.patreon.com/elizabethspanncraig .

I have Myrtle Clover tote bags, charms, magnets, and other goodies at my Café Press shop: https://www.cafepress.com/cozymystery

If you'd like an autographed book for yourself or a friend, please visit my Etsy page.

I'd also like to thank some folks who helped me put this book together. Thanks to my cover designer, Karri Klawiter, for her awesome covers. Thanks to my editor, Judy Beatty, for all of her help. Thanks to beta readers Amanda Arrieta and Dan Harris for all of their helpful suggestions and careful reading. Thanks, as always, to my family and readers.

Other Works by the Author:

Myrtle Clover Series in Order (be sure to look for the Myrtle series in audio, ebook, and print):

Pretty is as Pretty Dies

Progressive Dinner Deadly

A Dyeing Shame

A Body in the Backyard

Death at a Drop-In

A Body at Book Club

Death Pays a Visit

A Body at Bunco

Murder on Opening Night

Cruising for Murder

Cooking is Murder

A Body in the Trunk

Cleaning is Murder

Edit to Death (2019)

Southern Quilting Mysteries in Order:

Quilt or Innocence

Knot What it Seams

Quilt Trip

Shear Trouble

Tying the Knot

Patch of Trouble

Fall to Pieces

Rest in Pieces

On Pins and Needles

Fit to be Tied (2019)

The Village Library Mysteries in Order (Debuting 2019):

Checked Out (2019)

Memphis Barbeque Mysteries in Order (Written as Riley Adams):

Delicious and Suspicious

Finger Lickin' Dead

Hickory Smoked Homicide

Rubbed Out

And a standalone "cozy zombie" novel: Race to Refuge, written as Liz Craig